WITCH AND FAMOUS

A WESTWICK WITCHES COZY MYSTERY

COLLEEN CROSS

SLICE PUBLISHING

ALSO BY COLLEEN CROSS

Westwick Witches Cozy Mysteries

Witch You Well

Rags to Witches

Witch and Famous

Christmas Witch List

Witching Hour Dead

Witching for Love on Valentines Day

Katerina Carter Fraud Legal Thrillers

Exit Strategy

Game Theory

Blowout

Greenwash

Red Handed

Blue Moon

Nonfiction

Anatomy of a Ponzi Scheme

Lights, camera, assassin...

A Hollywood movie shoot comes to town and journalist Cendrine West is eager for a scoop. Her witchy family also wants in on the action, but shenanigans with the stars soon turn to Tinseltown tragedy.

Bodies are piling up faster than a coven's worth of curses, and everything points back to Cen's starstruck family. They will stop at nothing in their quest for supernatural stardom, even if that means meddling in a murder investigation.

The witches have created one spell of a mess and given the killer a chance to get away with murder. Cen resorts to her own blend of supernatural justice to keep her family in check, but can she unmask the killer before he strikes again?

Welcome to the wild, wild Wests!

Witch & Famous is for fans of paranormal mystery, cozy mystery, and wickedly funny witches.

This book can be read as a standalone mystery, but if you want to know more about the Westwick Witches and their family history, you can start with book 1: *Witch You Well.*

CHAPTER 1

$\mathcal{M}$ovie stars can be cantankerous, demanding creatures. I just never expected Aunt Amber to be any of those things. Not only was she an accomplished witch; she was also used to getting her way as a senior executive with Witches International Community Craft Association. WICCA was her life.

Yet my workaholic aunt had abandoned her career for an acting role. She had never expressed an interest in acting and didn't even like going to the movies, so the idea of her starring in a major Hollywood blockbuster was preposterous.

Yet in less than a week she had landed a co-starring role in *High Noon Heist*, the sequel to the mega-successful Hollywood blockbuster movie *Midnight Heist*. And convinced a hotshot Hollywood producer to film the movie right here in Westwick Corners. Our almost-ghost town could certainly use an economic boost, but I couldn't for the life of me figure out why our rundown town was chosen.

It made no sense. Either Aunt Amber had powerful Hollywood connections, had piled on the witchcraft, or both. The details were still sketchy, and I had no idea who was starring opposite Aunt Amber other than it was some Hollywood hotshot.

Why he was willing to travel all the way to eastern Washington State I had no idea. But one thing was clear: the film crew really was from Hollywood, and as long as things went well, the movie was pretty much guaranteed to put Westwick Corners back on the map. The tourists would return with their wallets and Westwick Corners would be financially in the black once more.

All my information came secondhand from Mom since I hadn't even seen Aunt Amber yet. She had arrived late last night from London, England, where she now lived. She had gone straight to her dressing-room trailer downtown instead of stopping in to see us. That seemed a little odd, but in typical Aunt Amber fashion, she was eager to get a head start.

Mom and I had spent all night readying our family's bed and breakfast, The Westwick Corners Inn, for our incoming guests. Even witches couldn't escape a certain amount of manual labor. There just weren't enough hours in the day, or night in this case. I had tumbled into bed around 1 a.m. but I tossed and turned.

My mind churned as I mentally ran through the details. The rooms were ready and Mom had the dining room tables set for breakfast. I would hang around the set as a sort of town liaison, making sure the film bigwigs had everything they needed. I also hoped to interview some of the stars for *The Westwick Corners Weekly*. I was the paper's publisher, though that sounded more impressive than it actually was. In reality, I had bought myself the job when the previous owner retired. I realized soon enough that it was a newspaper with dying circulation and probably not the best business to be in these days. As Aunt Pearl liked to say, it was just a free newspaper for coupon clippers.

Her comments stung but she was right. My dedicated coupon clippers didn't give a hoot about the articles I spent hours writing. Thinking otherwise bordered on insanity. My ever-shrinking pool of aging pensioners just wanted coupons and sale flyers. But at least for now, the advertising revenue still paid the bills and kept my newspaper afloat.

My only other assignment was to keep an eye on Aunt Pearl. That was easier said than done. Aunt Pearl hated the idea of visitors coming to town. She also had an intense sibling rivalry with Aunt Amber, so I hoped they could just get along for once.

I glanced at the clock and saw that it was just before 5 a.m. I felt like I hadn't slept a wink all night, and it was obvious I wasn't going to fall back asleep. I was too excited about the movie. It seemed too good to be true. There had to be witchcraft involved, and I was afraid the spell would be broken at any moment.

I pulled on jeans and a t-shirt and headed outside. I skipped down the treehouse steps, breathing in the moist morning air. My grandfather had built the treehouse years ago at the far end of the property overlooking the vineyard. It was private but also only a few hundred yards away from the Inn where Mom and Aunt Pearl lived on the bottom floor.

I turned my thoughts back to Aunt Amber. She was definitely up to something, but what? Maybe she was just trying to help business by bringing the movie to Westwick Corners.

Or maybe not. I hadn't known her to do anything that wasn't self-promoting in some way. She already had the movie role, so why did the film have to be shot here? Something niggled at my brain just out of grasp. Aunt Amber wouldn't take a leave of absence from WICCA for anything—unless magic was involved. Yet there were no telltale signs, or at least none that I could see.

A more accomplished witch would easily recognize supernatural hijinks but I was remiss with my spells. I always meant to practice more, but life just seemed to get in the way. Especially lately. As things heated up between me and Tyler, everything else seemed to take a back seat. The thought of my hunky boyfriend made me smile. Tyler Gates was also our town sheriff. He would be busy today too, with all the movie people in town.

I planned to check in on Aunt Amber at her trailer and see what else I could find out. The Inn was quiet and dark as I walked by, our guests not yet awake for breakfast. That was still a few hours away. I had lots of time to check out the movie set on Main Street.

I walked down the hill, enjoying the early morning quiet. It was still dark, so I used a flashlight to find my way along the tree-lined driveway that wound its way down the hill. I reached the main road that led downtown and headed towards Main Street. As I got closer I saw figures busily moving back and forth across the street. Apparently, the movie crew had been up all night too.

The normally deserted streets stirred with activity as crews unloaded trucks, set up lighting and equipment. Mobile dressing room trailers were parked on the opposite side of the bank building. I scanned the street for my redheaded aunt, but saw no sign of her. I figured she was inside her trailer.

I headed towards the set, which was technically just the two center blocks of Westwick Corner's Main Street. Brick and stone buildings from the start of the 20th century lined the street. The three-story bank building was the tallest building in town and the setting for the first scene in *High Noon Heist*. All sorts of cameras, lights and equipment were set up around the building as dozens of people scurried back and forth.

Filming in Westwick Corners certainly had some advantages. The buildings had basically remained untouched for decades. There was simply no money to renovate or build new ones. Main Street was quite picturesque in a faded and forgotten sort of way. The neglected buildings still sported the same windows and trim from the turn of the last century. Things looked exactly as they had then, only shabbier. Visitors to our town often said that it was like stepping back in time.

Except that now the brick was sandblasted, the wood trim freshly coated with paint, and the buildings sported signage from the 1900s era. Even the asphalt road was covered with six inches of dirt so that it now resembled a dirt road.

All this had happened overnight. I couldn't believe it was just the film crew's work. No doubt Aunt Amber's supernatural touch was somehow involved. However it had happened, our spruced-up town's facelift put a smile on my face.

The few traces of modernity had been either disguised or removed. It seemed that our almost-bankrupt town's financial problems had been solved overnight. The movie had paid our town handsomely for the shoot, and the cast and crew brought money to Westwick Corners too. We even had guests at our Inn, and other local businesses also benefited. The movie and the town's facelift could even put our town back in the black again.

I headed to Mom's food truck parked a half-block away. It was a hastily conjured up 1960s-era panel truck with lettering on the side that read *Ruby's Burgers*. Below the lettering was an open counter that revealed a full stainless steel kitchen inside. As I approached, the side door opened and Mom emerged.

I was surprised to see her here in town and not at the Inn, but sometimes witches could be in two places at the same time. Or rather, they appeared to be. It was an illusion but a pretty effective one.

"Cen, have you seen Amber?" Mom brushed flour off the daisy-covered apron that covered her tie-dye shirt and faded embroidered jeans. She always dressed like a modern-day hippie but somehow looked fashionable at the same time. Her quirky fashion sense was completely unplanned. She never threw anything away and just liked to dress comfortably.

I shook my head. "That's who I'm looking for. I was just heading over to check her dressing room trailer." I also hoped to get a sense of where the other stars' trailers were. Maybe I could interview a few of them before filming started.

"Tell her to drop by when she has a chance. I need someone to watch over things for a while." That was Mom's code for babysitting Aunt Pearl so she wouldn't ruin things with her mischief. Aunt Pearl hated tourists, even though they brought money to our town. This movie thing was sure to fray her nerves.

While Mom could be in two places at the same time, so to speak, it was a bit much to tend to the Inn, work the catering truck, and watch Aunt Pearl at the same time. Even with her split-second speed, it was too long to leave Aunt Pearl unsupervised. Mom's witchcraft skills were a decided advantage when it came to getting a head start on the catering competition, but they paled in comparison to Aunt Pearl's talents. And my aunt tended not to channel her skills productively.

Mom waved her hand towards the seating area around the trailer. "What do you think?"

A dozen or so round tables with chairs were set up to the right of the truck, under the shade of a large willow tree. The tables looked inviting with red-checkered tablecloths and vases of white and red carnations gracing each table. Mom's plan was to get everything ready at the catering truck for mid-morning snacks and lunch, then head back to the Inn and serve breakfast to the guests.

"Looks like you have everything covered. Need any help with the food prep?" Not that she needed it—her cooking was to die for.

But die we might, with ornery Aunt Pearl manning the barbecue. She emerged from the trailer and headed to the barbecue area. It was to the left of the food truck, about ten feet away.

"Keep out of it, Cen. I've got everything under control." Aunt Pearl reversed course and headed towards us, brandishing barbecue tongs like a weapon.

I was about to ask why she was barbecuing so early in the morning when Mom caught my eye. She pressed a finger to her lips to silence me. The burgers would be wasted, but that was a small price to pay in order to keep Aunt Pearl occupied.

"Cen, you're just in time for lunch. Grab a bun." Aunt Pearl motioned to a rectangular table beside the food truck. It was laden with buns, condiments, and salads. "These are my secret recipe char-broiled burgers."

"It's not even breakfast time yet," I protested. "How about a coffee instead?"

She ignored me and turned away, strangely oblivious to the three-foot flames that shot up behind her from the barbecue. The flames came awfully close to the willow tree branches that hung low overhead.

"Watch out!" The tree's lower branches smoked and crackled as sparks flew. I looked around for something to douse the flames, but Mom was one step ahead of me. She whispered a few words and within seconds the barbecue flames were extinguished.

Pyromaniac Aunt Pearl loved an audience and would go to great lengths for attention. It usually involved magic, fire, or too often, both. She especially loved to irritate me, so I wanted to ignore her. But I couldn't when safety was at stake. I glanced over at the film set workers. Thankfully they were all too immersed in their tasks to notice the split-second flare-up.

"Relax, Cen. I would have fixed anything that got out of hand. You always overreact."

"It's better if nothing happens in the first place." I studied the plate of blackened burgers on the table beside her. "Nobody's going to eat those things. They're burnt to a crisp."

Mom swooped up the plate. "Some people like their burgers well done. I'll just take these inside so they're ready to go."

Those burgers were headed for the trash, but Aunt Pearl didn't know that. I mentally calculated the number of burgers per hour that my Aunt could barbecue before noon. It was an expensive way to keep the peace, but at least it kept other damage to a minimum. Aunt Pearl could really wreak havoc if she wanted to. At least on burger detail, she was under Mom's watchful eyes.

I was scared to think of what other little disasters Aunt Pearl had planned to stop filming. Despite her helpful demeanor, I knew she wanted nothing more than to run these interlopers out of town. I hated to think of what plans she had for our fully booked Inn, where she was chief housekeeper.

That job was Mom's idea, thinking it would mean limited to no interaction with guests. Unfortunately though, it gave Aunt Pearl unfettered access to the guest rooms, and unlimited opportunities for mischief with shampoo, soap and charging weird cable shows to the guests' accounts. She probably had much worse ideas in mind, but ignorance is bliss and I didn't want to even think about what else was going on in that head of hers.

The more immediate problem was Aunt Pearl's barbecue antics. I was afraid to ask, but did anyway. "What are you doing here? I thought Aunt Amber got you a job on set." Were they fighting already?

Aunt Pearl ignored me as she slapped another half dozen burgers onto the grill. She turned up the gas.

Aunt Amber had promised to keep her oldest sister occupied 24/7. Yet Aunt Pearl was here in the thick of things just waiting to stir up trouble. She was a ninety-pound tornado just looking for a place to land. Tourists, movie people—they were all the enemy in her mind. Her presence at Mom's food truck was no coincidence. I just hoped she wouldn't go so far as to poison people.

"Amber got Pearl a great job working with props, but Pearl refuses to take it." Mom tucked a stray blonde hair under her bright fuchsia and turquoise bandana. "Says it's beneath her."

"You got it wrong, Ruby. I never refused." Aunt Pearl waved her barbecue fork in the air, almost spearing a tree branch. "The job was misrepresented to me. I was supposed to be the head of pyrotechnics, not some lackey guarding a toy box. No wonder Amber's avoiding me. She's going to pay for this."

"You can't be the head of pyrotechnics. You don't have any movie experience." I sighed. My aunts' sibling rivalry knew no bounds. "I'm sure Aunt Amber was just trying to help."

Aunt Pearl snorted as she sprinkled liquid from her hip flask onto the barbecue. Flames shot up from the grill a split-second later. She gazed lovingly at the flames as they rose higher and higher from the grill. She seemed to be in a trance.

"Watch out!" The hair on the back of my neck rose. My five-foot-nothing firebug aunt had a hate-on for authority figures, both formal and informal. She was also a recovering pyromaniac, so the idea of her having anything to do with fire freaked me out.

The flames lessened as the fuel burned off, and Aunt Pearl came out of her trance. "You said something?" She smiled sweetly at us.

"Props is a great opportunity, Pearl. You've got to start somewhere." Mom turned the barbecue flame down. "You can add that experience to your résumé."

"Amber doesn't have experience." Aunt Pearl snorted. "How come she gets a leading role?"

I wondered that too. Instead, I said, "You're just jealous."

"Am not."

I rolled my eyes. "Do you always have to compete with each other?" Mom's two older sisters were now in their sixties and seventies, with Aunt Pearl the oldest. Their intense sibling rivalry hadn't diminished at all. In fact, it had grown stronger with each passing year. They couldn't be in the same room for five minutes before they tried to one-up each other. Mom always broke up their spats and played mediator even though she was the youngest.

"I wish you and Amber would stop being so competitive," Mom said. "You're both good at different things, that's all. You complement each other."

I snorted involuntarily and they both glared at me.

"I have life experience, Ruby. I'm also a witch and a darn good one too. I'm not about to work for some incompetent has-been who doesn't know what the heck he's doing."

"You mean the props manager? Of course he knows what he's doing. He's got years of experience like everyone else here. They're all professionals." Mom tilted her head in the direction of the set.

"I can whip up some mean special effects. His are a joke." Aunt Pearl waved her hand and the barbecue flames shot up again.

Mom shot them down with a wave of her hand. "Just keep a lid on your tricks for a couple of days, okay? None of the movie people know we're witches and we have to keep it that way."

"But Bill doesn't know what he's doing. At this rate, they'll be filming forever." She scowled. "I just wanted to lend a helping hand so they can wrap things up quickly. But whatever I suggest gets shot down."

"Don't try any funny stuff, Aunt Pearl." I had no idea who Bill was or why she called him incompetent, but I figured anyone working on a movie this big had to be good at his job. More likely, excellent at it. Movie making was an industry everyone wanted to be in, and competition for jobs was fierce.

"Cen's right. You can't blow our cover," Mom said. "Just do good work and earn their respect. At least Amber got you a job."

Aunt Pearl shook her head. "No can do. I won't compromise on quality. I have standards, you know."

I had no idea what quality standards she was talking about. Maybe another job was just too stressful for her. Westwick Corners was so small that most locals had a few jobs. We all had to be entrepreneurs because the local economy was nonexistent.

The West family was no different since we all pitched in to run the Westwick Corners Inn and our bar, The Witching Post, in addition to other jobs. We always needed extra money to make ends meet. That was probably why Aunt Amber had gotten us all involved in the movie in the first place.

Everyone except me, that is. I felt a little slighted that Aunt Amber hadn't gotten me a job too, but in another sense I was relieved. Most West family ventures tended to go haywire. I could just watch from a distance.

But still.

Why not me? Was it because I didn't practice my witchcraft enough? True, I was a Pearl's Charm School dropout, but punishing me for being a slacker witch seemed extreme. Maybe Aunt Amber didn't think I was good enough, but trusting Aunt Pearl for a job ahead of me was both surprising and disturbing. Maybe it was Aunt Amber's way of giving me a wake-up call, but her tough love approach hurt.

I watched as Aunt Pearl flipped charcoal-black burgers off the grill and onto a plate. She promptly dropped another half dozen burgers on the grill.

"Maybe you shouldn't work on the movie after all. What will your students do?" Pearl's Charm School, Aunt Pearl's witchcraft school, had zero students and was foundering, despite Aunt Pearl's claims to the contrary. In fact, all of our businesses were in serious trouble, including The Westwick Corners Weekly. The movie shoot was the biggest thing to come to town in decades, and we all wanted—no, needed—to be a part of it.

"I need a break from teaching. You know how I get bored," Aunt Pearl snapped. "Those students really test my patience sometimes too."

"How is this any better?" I studied my gray-haired aunt. "You're flipping burgers on a barbecue. And you're miserable about it."

"It's not better at all, Cendrine. That's kind of the point," Aunt Pearl sniffed. "The special effects role was supposed to provide me with an outlet for my creative juices. Amber promised me full creative control. She said that if I helped her land the movie, she'd make it worth my while. Then she belittled me by getting me a job way below my talents and capabilities."

I was tempted to ask how exactly she had helped Aunt Amber arrange for the movie to be filmed in Westwick Corners, but our discussion was already getting sidetracked.

"You can't use witchcraft. Or fire." I had a sinking feeling that whatever help Aunt Pearl had given came with strings attached. Some things were better not knowing.

"You know I wouldn't do that, Cendrine." Aunt Pearl's lower lip stuck out in a fake pout and her eye twitched the way it always did when she was lying. "I always follow the rules."

I bit my tongue, not wanting to start an argument. Aunt Pearl had probably steamrolled Aunt Amber into the props job by threatening something worse. Her disappointment only meant that we could expect more revenge of some kind. What the retaliation would be wasn't exactly clear, but we all dreaded Aunt Pearl's bouts of "creativity". There was a fine line between giving in to her demands and keeping her out of trouble. No wonder Aunt Amber had gotten her the props assistant role.

That was also why Mom had her manning the barbecue. If Aunt Pearl was going to play with fire, at least it would be supervised.

$\mathcal{M}$om and I reluctantly left Aunt Pearl at the catering truck while we tended to breakfast at the Inn. It was rare to have our boutique bed and breakfast fully booked like it was today. Most of the cast and crew had opted for more modern accommodations an hour away in Shady Creek, but some had decided to stay in town. Our guests included a few VIPs and we wanted to pull out all the stops to make a great impression. We hoped to encourage return visits and maybe even garner some free publicity.

I grated cheese for omelets while Mom chopped vegetables. We were just settling into a rhythm when a shrill voice interrupted us.

"How could you leave me alone here to fend for myself?" Grandma Vi's ghostly form flitted back and forth across the kitchen. "I don't like all these intruders. What are they doing here?"

"They're filming a movie, Grandma. It's only temporary." I was surprised that Aunt Amber hadn't told her in advance about the movie, but then again, Aunt Amber hadn't given any of us much notice.

"I don't have a few days. I want you to get rid of all these people." Her apparition wavered the way it did when she got really upset.

Grandma never forgave Mom for turning our family home into a boutique bed and breakfast, and this was just the icing on the cake.

"You're a ghost, Grandma. You've got all the time in the world." Grandma stayed with me in the treehouse now. While a ghostly roommate seemed like an ideal situation, Grandma Vi was really hard to live with. She constantly competed for my attention when I had guests over and complained of loneliness when it was just the two of us.

"Don't keep reminding me. At least put the house back the way it was."

She meant the Inn, which was unchanged except for the presence of guests. "We have to earn a living somehow, Grandma. They'll be gone soon." I felt bad but our cash needs outweighed her feelings for the moment. Either we rented out the rooms or we moved to another town with job opportunities.

"Soon is a couple of days too long for me. I'm trying to be patient but they've already overstayed their welcome. I've had enough of this. Time to make a spectacle of myself." She headed towards the door that led out into the dining room.

I raced to the door and blocked it with my body. "Specter, Grandma. You're a specter, not a spectacle. Please don't go in there. I'll make it up to you somehow, I promise." I glanced over at Mom, but her back was turned as she cooked breakfast on the grill.

"You know I can pass right through you, Cen." She floated six inches from my face. "Don't make me do it."

"Okay, fine. Why don't we make some tinctures later on?" Bribery was the only weapon I had. Grandma could wreak havoc if she didn't get her way. "We haven't done that in a while."

Grandma's aura immediately brightened to a happy sunny yellow. "I would love that. We'll make love potions and bewitch all these movie people." She giggled like a teenager. "Think of the trouble we'll start!"

"That sounds like fun!" My voice came out a little higher pitched than normal, so I hoped I sounded convincing. I had no intention of using magic on the movie people without their knowledge, but Grandma Vi didn't have to know that. "Maybe we can do it tomorrow, once things settle down a bit."

She shook her head slowly. "No. You'll have to think of something better than that. What am I supposed to do in the meantime?"

"Why don't you pick out some shows and movies to watch? We can binge-watch all the old *Bewitched* and *I Dream of Jeannie* episodes tonight. Just to get inspired." I reached out to pat her arm, but naturally my hand went right through her.

"That's all you've got to offer? That's hardly worth my while," Grandma Vi said. "Besides, I'm not really in the mood for comedy. In fact, I wouldn't mind blowing off some steam and scaring some people right now. Maybe I'll create my own drama."

"Please don't, Grandma." I held up my hand in protest. It was obvious where Aunt Pearl got her ornery attitude from, but it was also clear that Grandma Vi had been pushed too far. I lowered my voice to a whisper so that Mom couldn't hear. "Maybe we could do a spell on Amber and Pearl. You know, so they get along better."

"Hmmm." She floated up towards the ceiling, deep in thought. A couple of seconds later she popped up two inches in front of me. "That's a very good idea, Cen. You'll learn something new, and my daughters can get along for once."

"Deal," I said. "I'll get some herbs from the garden and see you back at the treehouse later tonight." Making tinctures was the only part of witchcraft I was really comfortable with, though I doubted there was a potion strong enough to take the edges off my aunts' strong personalities. It seemed to satisfy Grandma Vi, at least for the moment.

"Ta ta." Grandma Vi's image faded into nothing.

I turned my thoughts back to Aunt Pearl. Leaving her unsupervised around the movie people was risky, but we didn't have much choice. At least it was still early morning, a time when she was usually in a more civil mood and less likely to act up. The barbecue had satisfied her inner fire bug for the time being.

We needed two people at the Inn, one to cook and one to serve breakfast. As the server, I had an ulterior motive, which was to arrange interviews with some of our more famous guests. Then maybe, just maybe, one of my articles would catch on with readers and I could really make a go of it. I had several articles already planned on the movie shoot and write-ups on the movie stars. All I needed was to actually meet some of them while I served breakfast.

What I wanted more than anything was to meet Steven Scarabelli, the legendary producer who was staying at our inn. But that wasn't to be, at least not yet. It turned out that I missed him by mere minutes as he had skipped breakfast and departed for the set while we were cooking.

Fortunately, it didn't take Mom and me long to attend to the guests and we were soon headed back to the food truck. Main Street bustled with activity and even more buildings had been painted while we were away. The street's fresh new facades contrasted sharply with the side streets. There the neglected buildings remained boarded, paint peeling from their wooden facades.

I felt a surge of hope, satisfied that the movie had already breathed new life into Westwick Corners even though filming hadn't started yet. Our town's population had dwindled from thousands to just a few hundred over the last decade, and the lack of jobs drove young people away as soon as they finished school. Some went to nearby Shady Creek, and others went even further afield to Seattle. But the movie could reverse that tide. Now our luck was about to change for the better.

If the movie people liked our town, they would return. We could brand ourselves as a Hollywood North of sorts. The movie was a huge economic boost, a golden opportunity that had dropped in our laps. One movie could lead to another, and bring with it jobs and cash. Witches could do a lot of things, but we couldn't conjure up money. Success was ours as long as we didn't squander it.

I was jarred from my thoughts as we neared the food truck. A flash of red caught my eye. It was so bright that it reflected off the white truck and I had to shield my eyes. As I got closer I saw the source. A platinum blonde bombshell in a red sequined evening gown posed in front of the food truck.

At first, I thought it was one of the actresses, but as we drew closer I saw that wasn't the case. A sick feeling formed in the pit of my stomach.

Mom saw it too. "Oh no! I told Pearl that Carolyn was not welcome here. Why does she always have to ruin things?"

I didn't have an answer. Carolyn Conroe was Aunt Pearl's alter ego, a thirtyish Marilyn Monroe lookalike creation that Aunt Pearl shape-shifted into whenever she craved attention. Especially male attention.

Aunt Pearl claimed that she hated men, but simultaneously seemed to be living out some weird fantasy vicariously through Carolyn Conroe. I was embarrassed to watch, though everyone else seemed oblivious to her shenanigans.

Her skintight sequined dress strained at her curves as she balanced a plateful of burgers stacked a foot high. She beckoned like a siren song to the steady stream of male admirers who walked almost zombie-like towards the food truck. I counted at least two dozen, none of them locals so I assumed they were part of the film crew. I doubted there was much work being done at the moment.

Carolyn had brought the film set to a standstill, baited with beef and blonde hair. If we were to impress the Hollywood bigwigs, we had to avoid disruptions like this. Our future depended upon the movie going off without a hitch.

As we got closer I got a good look at Carolyn's admirers. A few of them were practically drooling as they stared at her, trance-like. "At least we know what she's up to."

"True," Mom said. "And this way we can keep her away from Amber. Their competitiveness could get out of hand and ruin everything."

I nodded. A supernatural beauty contest was the last thing we needed, with each sister trying to outdo the other. Mostly it was Aunt Pearl who instigated things. She resented the fact that her younger sister was better-looking and had a much more successful career.

I was surprised that Aunt Pearl would dare to pull her Carolyn Conroe act with Aunt Amber nearby. Technically her shape shifting was a violation of WICCA rules. There were very few instances where a witch was allowed to impersonate someone, real or imagined. While Aunt Pearl constantly broke rules, she was already two strikes out of three from an incident earlier in the year. As a WICCA VP, Aunt Amber was a stickler for rules. The last thing we needed was a showdown.

"I'm going to find Aunt Amber. I need to talk to her." I scanned the street and was relieved to see no sign of her. At least I could track her down before she saw Carolyn.

Carolyn sat on one the tables in the eating area, posed suggestively with a generous glimpse of skin peeking out from the thigh-high slit of her evening gown.

I couldn't leave Mom alone with her like this.

The number of tables had doubled while we were away, obviously more of Aunt Pearl's magical antics meant to lure men. They were laden with burgers, sandwiches, salads, and cold drinks. A few of the men helped themselves to snacks, but most just stood in awe of Carolyn, blissfully unaware that they had been duped. That was quite a feat when you thought about it, since the film crew saw gorgeous Hollywood actresses on set all the time.

I walked over to Carolyn's table and slipped my arm into hers. I steered her away from her male admirers. "Why are you doing this? You're messing up the filming schedule."

Carolyn's crimson-stained mouth formed into an innocent-looking O as she touched her fingers to her lips. "I'm not doing a thing. I can't help it if those men are hungry."

"They're not hungry. They're—never mind." I glared at her. "You don't fool me, Aunt Pearl. I know what you're up to."

"Stop calling me that—my name's Carolyn. And I haven't the faintest idea what you're talking about." She plumped her platinum blonde hair with a manicured hand. Her nails sported the exact crimson red shade as her lipstick and dress. "Oh, I get it. You must have talked to Amber. Now I can't even cook? She's obviously jealous and worried that I'll upstage her."

"No, I haven't even seen Aunt Amber yet, but I doubt she's jealous of you. Now change back to your normal self before I do something drastic."

"Oh, stop complaining, Cendrine. Let me have a little fun for once. At least you have a job that suits you."

Mom re-emerged from the trailer, sensing trouble. She sidled up beside Carolyn, so that only I could see her expression. She rolled her eyes but didn't say anything.

I knew better than to fall for one of Aunt Pearl's distraction techniques but I couldn't help myself. "Why all of a sudden do you think my job suits me? You called my newspaper a dead-end job."

"It is a dead-end just like your life." Carolyn shrugged. "You have no ambition for anything greater. You won't practice your witchcraft, you settled for that no-good sheriff as a boyfriend, and you're just plain difficult. You should know this by now but I'll say it again: you only reap what you sow."

As if on cue, I spotted Sheriff Tyler Gates walking briskly towards us. As he got closer, I saw that my normally calm boyfriend was angry, his usual smile replaced by a frown. He wasn't the only one worked up today.

I turned back to Aunt Pearl, my face flushed in anger. "Just because I don't want to go to Pearl's Charm School doesn't make me a dead-beat. Your distractions aren't going to work either. You know how important this movie is to the whole town. Can't you just be yourself for once?"

"No, not like that—" Mom stopped in mid-sentence as flames shot up from the barbecue.

"Uh-oh," Carolyn's hand flew to her mouth, "Help!"

I pulled her away from the barbecue as flames shot up ten feet in the air. "Aunt Pearl!"

"I told you not to call me—"

I ignored her and steered her away. "You're going to set the whole town on fire."

Two of the men who were standing nearby tore their shirts off and raced over to the barbecue. Together they smothered the flames.

"Oh my!" Aunt Pearl swooned in her best Scarlett O'Hara imitation.

One of the men rushed to Carolyn's side. "Are you all right, miss?" He placed a protective arm around her and guided her away from the barbecue.

"What about us?" Mom turned to me.

"I guess we're invisible." I studied the charred remains of the barbecue, wondering how many times this was going to happen today.

"Hardly." Tyler put his arm around me. He knew our family secret, which made being a witch a little easier. "I think you'd better find Pearl a new job though. Something without access to accelerants."

Mom shook her head. "I don't know what to do, Tyler. She refuses to do the job Amber got for her, and she can't work with me if she's going to mess with the food. The way she lit up that barbecue..."

"Leave it with me. I'll figure something out," I said. "And I'll keep an eye on her too."

"Good," Tyler said. "Because Brayden's watching me like a hawk. And he's promised to have my head if anything goes wrong." Brayden Banks was our town mayor and my former fiancé. He resented the fact that Tyler and I were dating and constantly looked for any excuse to fire Tyler.

"He just wants to stir up trouble." I felt sorry for Tyler. He couldn't win no matter what. If there was any trouble during the movie shoot, Brayden would find a way to blame Tyler. If it was a success, Brayden would take all the credit.

I turned my attention back to Aunt Pearl and her employment status. I had to keep her occupied, but how? A master witch like Aunt Pearl could do a lot of damage, and her antics could prevent more movies from coming to Westwick Corners in the future. That wasn't good for any of us.

All things considered, Aunt Amber's idea of a job on set was probably our best bet, important because of Aunt Pearl's short fuse. I could supervise her and watch the filming at the same time. The props job also had limited interaction with other people. I just had to convince Aunt Pearl that the job was just as important as Aunt Amber's acting role.

"I'll talk to Aunt Amber," I said. "I'm sure we can work something out."

We could fight fire with fire after all.

CHAPTER 3

I couldn't help feeling a bit smug as I watched Aunt Pearl trudge slowly down the street towards home. After casting a forgetfulness spell to erase her short-term memory, I sent her on a fake errand to Pearl's Charm School. That would give me a little time to track down Aunt Amber to get Aunt Pearl's prop assistant job back.

Only this time, I would plant a false memory that it had been Aunt Pearl's idea in the first place. I felt a bit guilty until I remembered that Aunt Pearl did stuff like this to me all the time. So much for her poor opinion of my witchcraft skills. While I considered myself a reluctant witch, I had been secretly practicing my craft over the last few months. It was finally starting to pay off.

The forgetfulness spell was tricky because any other people involved had to be bewitched too. My aunt's male admirers now remembered arriving at the food truck only to find it closed with no one around. It was a tough intermediate spell, one I had only practiced a couple of times. I hadn't executed it perfectly, but I had come pretty close.

I had just outwitted a master witch with a spell of my very own. Needless to say, I was mighty proud of myself.

My spell had erased the last ten minutes of her life. The tables of food, the men…all gone. Even Carolyn was gone. Aunt Pearl had also spontaneously changed back into her crotchety old self. The only remaining evidence of Carolyn's burger carnage was the charred barbecue, something Mom could easily fix in a jiffy. Aunt Pearl would be proud of me—and furious to be the subject of my spell.

Aunt Pearl acted like a two-year-old in a seventy-year-old body sometimes. Her Carolyn alter ego was really just her way of acting out. We had worried that she might either attract too much guest attention—as Carolyn—or repel them, as her ornery self.

I guess I should have anticipated her boredom since Mom and I had temporarily taken over her housekeeping job at the Inn and left her with too much time on her hands. Too much time to get into trouble. And too much time to mull over Aunt Amber's movie role. No wonder she was upset. I felt partly to blame.

I decided to grab a coffee from the food truck before heading to the film set. I had just turned around when I felt a swoosh of air at my back.

"Cendrine!" Aunt Amber suddenly materialized in front of me, blocking my path to a much-needed caffeine fix. Her red hair was pulled back to show off an expensive-looking pair of diamond drop earrings and a matching necklace. Even in her silk dressing gown, she had all the glamor of a 1950's movie star.

Except that the movie was a 1900s-era Western. Her diamonds and high heels seemed totally inappropriate for the dusty street. "Shouldn't you be getting ready for your scene?"

She waved her hand dismissively. "I urgently need your help. I can't find my assistant."

"That's too bad." I decided to forgo the coffee and headed towards the set. I stepped over electrical cables as I scanned the street, half-expecting a horse-drawn Cinderella carriage to come to Aunt Amber's rescue. Luckily nothing like that happened, but a few of the men from Carolyn's damsel in distress barbecue drama were milling around nearby. They didn't seem to notice us.

"Maybe Aunt Pearl could help you. She should be back any minute."

Aunt Amber snorted. "You can't be serious. She's got the attention span of a gnat. I need someone detail-oriented. Someone I can trust to do a good job."

I looked around. "I'll keep an eye out for your assistant."

"Someone like you." Aunt Amber shoved an armful of dresses into my arms, almost knocking me over. "Take these things to my trailer. I'll need them pressed and ready in an hour."

"I'm sorry, Aunt Amber. I don't have time." I tried to push the dresses back but she just pushed back harder. I teetered for a moment before I recovered my balance. I leaned into her with all my weight but she didn't budge.

"Make time, Cendrine. This is important."

"I'm sure your assistant will turn up sooner or later." At least Aunt Amber hadn't flaunted her witchy powers to get her dresses pressed. I turned back towards the food truck, but she blocked my path.

"I don't have time for this. Just take them already." She nodded in the general direction of the trailers.

I raised my arms in protest but she simply pushed my arms back down. The full-length dresses were made of thick wool and were unbelievably heavy. I staggered backward from the weight.

"I promised Mom I'd help her with the after breakfast cleanup." I felt guilty lying but I didn't have the time or inclination to be Aunt Amber's wardrobe assistant. She never took no for an answer. The minute I said yes, she would assign me dozens of equally unpleasant tasks. I had to stand my ground.

"For crying out loud, Cen. We're witches. Just cast a spell."

"You could do the same," I pointed out. The dress on top was flouncy with several layers of petticoat. Aside from being unbelievably heavy, I could barely see in front of me. Every time I pushed down on the dress to see, it just poofed right back up again. I braced myself and shifted the dresses onto one shoulder so that I could at least see where I was going.

I scanned the street for someone to hand off Aunt Amber's clothing to, but everyone just ignored me as they scurried around like ants on speed. I was still troubled by how a sixty-something witch with no acting experience had landed a leading role in a major Hollywood movie. Something was fishy, and I wasn't sure I liked it.

"Just do it, okay? I've got to get ready for my robbery scene." She glared at me and adjusted the belt on her dressing gown.

"You can't go like that," I said. "You have to go to your trailer to change anyway, so why not take the dresses? Besides, I don't even know where your trailer is."

Too late. Aunt Amber ran behind a building and whispered in a low tone. Seconds later she emerged from her hiding place, clad in a 1900s-era long blue dress with a high lace collar. Her diamond jewelry was gone, but now she donned an elaborate white and blue hat and carried a matching parasol. She immediately disappeared through the doors of the old bank building without another word.

My arms ached, but I couldn't exactly leave the dresses lying around. They looked expensive and I didn't want them to get damaged. Maybe I could hand them off to someone on set. They would have somewhere to keep them safe. Aunt Amber's assistant would turn up sooner or later.

I needed my hands free so I could get a story, or maybe even a dozen stories before this movie shoot was over. I worried that once Aunt Amber's spell was broken, everything would end just as suddenly as it had begun. The movie execs had obviously been bewitched to even consider filming in our has-been town. The movie stars and the film crew would leave and we would return to barely eking out a living and passing time. I had to interview the stars before they realized their mistake and packed up and left.

I especially wanted to scoop an interview with the leading man. A stockpile of movie shoot stories might just keep The Westwick Corners Weekly afloat. All I needed was a few good stories to turn things around.

But to do that I had to get cracking, and that meant unloading the dresses. My spirits lifted as I neared the trailers on the opposite end of the set. Aunt Amber's trailer must be nearby.

"Need a hand?" A thirtyish man smiled at me and motioned for the dresses.

I gladly accepted and placed them in his arms. "Thanks. I'm supposed to take them to Amber West's trailer."

"Amber West?" The man frowned. "Don't recognize that name."

"Tall, slim, redhead about sixty years old?" *The witch that organized this crazy film shoot.*

He frowned, a puzzled expression on his face.

The co-star, I wanted to say, but stopped myself. Maybe she had lied or exaggerated. Who knew what was real and what wasn't?

"Amber West...oh yeah, right. Now I remember." He nodded towards another group of trailers parked further down Main Street in the vacant lot. "Her trailer's this way. C'mon, I'll show you."

I followed behind him, puzzled by his lack of familiarity with Aunt Amber, given she was a co-star and all. On the other hand, the whole movie shoot was a last-minute thing according to Mom. Aunt Amber had only been cast in her role yesterday after the original leading lady pulled out.

I followed him up the steps of a trailer decidedly smaller and older than the ones beside it. Aunt Amber's name was printed in block letters on a small white cardboard sign fastened to the door. It certainly didn't give the impression of a star, and there was no sign of an assistant. The trailer was empty.

"Here we are." The man dropped the clothes onto the foldout kitchen table and held out his hand. "Sorry, I didn't introduce myself. I'm Rick Mazure. The screenwriter."

I shook his hand. "Wow, you wrote *High Noon Heist*? And *Midnight Heist* too?"

He nodded.

"I'm Cendrine West. I'm a reporter for *The Westwick Corners Weekly.*" I omitted the fact that I was also the publisher, advertising manager, editor and chief coffee maker. "Thanks for going out of your way. I didn't know it would be a two-block walk."

"It's no trouble at all. I'm sure you'll find lots of juicy stories here, both on and off the set," Rick said. "I'd help you get started but I've got to run. I've got a deadline for some last-minute script rewrites, and some people around here get a little testy when things aren't finished yesterday."

I smiled. "I know exactly what you mean." I had no plans to wait for Aunt Amber so I followed him outside and watched him walk briskly back towards the set. I wanted to avoid small talk, and I was sure he did too. I waited until he was a half-block ahead and then headed in the same direction.

My office was near City Hall and the food truck, so the fastest way there was to cut back through the set. If I was lucky, I might run into one of the stars and wrangle an interview.

Westwick Corners had been transformed into an early 1900's Wild West town, or at least Hollywood's version of it. The set crew had multiplied in the last hour to the point that now it was bustling with old cars, horses, and period costumes. While I loved the freshly painted buildings, I kind of missed the town's former shabby splendor. It was like a favorite pair of jeans, worn and frayed in all the right places. Suddenly Westwick Corners seemed like a strange, sterile version of its former self.

The small supermarket parking lot across from the bank was filled with props, sets, and crew, who busily laid cables, erected lighting, and positioned props. A dozen or so men and women in period costumes were interspersed with the crew. The men all wore hats and the women wore long dresses, cinched alarmingly small at the waist.

I spotted Aunt Amber at the same time she saw me. She had somehow changed outfits again, this time into one of the period dresses I had just dropped off at her trailer. Witchcraft, of course. For someone so high up in WICCA, she certainly was flaunting the rules. I wondered how many she had broken to get this role.

"Cendrine! Help me with my lines." She ran towards me, holding her petticoats up from the dusty street.

"I told you, I'm late to help Mom." I lowered my voice. "You're a witch. You can memorize your lines in a snap." I snapped my fingers for emphasis.

"Great actors don't memorize lines. They become the character." She sniffed. "Every gesture, nuance, and inflection is critical. I need you to critique me. I'm the leading lady, so I have to get it right."

"I'm no acting expert, Aunt Amber. Maybe one of the other actors can help. Besides, I really need to go." I wanted to add that she shouldn't have waited until the last minute to practice her lines, but I didn't want her getting mad at me.

Aunt Amber sighed. "Okay, fine. But at least come and meet Steven with me." She plumped her hair with a hand. "He was so glad I convinced him to film here. Especially because the leading lady died suddenly, and he was in a pickle. He wants me to take her place."

"Wait—she died? I thought she quit." I had no idea that Aunt Amber had gotten the role because someone had died. Aunt Amber as the leading lady's replacement would already interest the locals since she had been born in Westwick Corners. Her predecessor's death made it all the more intriguing.

Aunt Amber waved her hand in dismissal. "Long story, doesn't matter right now. The important thing is that Steven says I have raw talent. He's going to make me a star!"

I glanced around at everyone scurrying about the set. I didn't see Steven Scarabelli, or anyone overseeing the activities for that matter. Everyone seemed to know exactly what to do, like they had done it a hundred times before. "Westwick Corners seems so low budget for him."

I wasn't a huge movie buff, but even I knew that Steven Scarabelli was a big deal. His films weren't quite as popular as they had been a few decades earlier, but they still won Oscars and Golden Globes. He was a Hollywood bigshot by anyone's standards, and actors seemed to love working with him.

"That's one of the reasons he chose it. He said it was so...authentic." Aunt Amber grabbed my hand. "Come with me and I'll introduce you."

CHAPTER 4

Ten minutes later, I sat beside Aunt Amber in Steven Scarabelli's office trailer. I was in awe of the legendary Hollywood director and producer, yet the man seated across from me seemed so ordinary, not at all like a Hollywood icon. His tired expression also made him appear much older than the man I had seen on television. He looked like he needed a good, long rest.

He stood and leaned over the desk. He shook my hand and gave me a warm, friendly smile. His casual attire of a white cotton shirt over dark jeans made him look more like a member of the crew instead of a top Hollywood director/producer.

"Welcome to Westwick Corners." It was lame but I didn't know what else to say. If any town had imposter syndrome, it was ours, hiding behind a fresh coat of paint. I was certain that Steven Scarabelli would come to his senses any moment now and call the whole thing off. We weren't exactly Hollywood material.

"It's great to be here. I would never have even known about this little gem if it weren't for Amber. Your aunt and I go way back." He nodded at Aunt Amber.

Aunt Amber beamed. "This movie's going to put our town on the map, Cen. *High Noon Heist* will be even bigger than *Midnight Heist* was. It's guaranteed to make a bundle for Steven and his investors."

"I'm counting on it." Steven Scarabelli pushed a contract towards Aunt Amber. "Here's the final contract for your signature. Everyone else has signed except for Dirk, who should be here any minute. Once I get his signature, we're good to go."

My mouth dropped open. Steven Scarabelli's last box-office blockbuster had starred one of Hollywood's biggest stars. "Dirk…as in Dirk Diamond? He's coming here to your trailer?" Men loved Dirk Diamond movies for the cheesy action plots. Women loved his movies for…well, Dirk Diamond.

Steven chuckled. "He better get here soon, or I'm in big trouble."

I was surprised that Steven hadn't already locked in his actors with signed contracts, but since this movie was a sequel maybe that was just a formality. Or maybe things were more informal in Hollywood. I somehow doubted that, but what did I know?

I turned to Aunt Amber. "Is Dirk staying in town?" I was really asking if he was one of our guests at The Westwick Corners Inn. I hadn't seen his name on the register, but then many stars checked in under fake names for anonymity.

"Of course," she said. "Steven's staying with us too, along with a few other cast members. The rest are staying in Shady Creek." She scribbled her signature on the contract and pushed it across the table to Steven and smiled at him. "There. I'm yours."

Steven grinned. "I just checked myself in at your property late last night. It looks lovely."

Our quaint and cozy inn wasn't anything close to a posh Beverly Hills hotel. It was probably a step down from what Steven was used to staying in, so it was very gracious of him to compliment us. I just hoped that he wouldn't be disappointed. The nearest luxury accommodations were an hour away in Shady Creek, so I guess convenience had won out over luxury.

"Our little town is going to be famous, Cen!" Amber rose and motioned for me to follow. "C'mon, I'll show you the set."

I imagined movie buffs making pilgrimages to Westwick Corners, spending money and staying at our Inn. I followed my aunt outside, glad her mood had improved. We screeched to a stop after almost colliding with a petite dark-haired woman. I apologized as she passed us and stepped into Steven's trailer.

I pointed excitedly. "That's Arianne Duval! Another Hollywood A-lister!"

Aunt Amber slapped my hand down. "Don't point, Cen! You're embarrassing me in front of my colleagues."

I turned to Aunt Amber. "How exactly did you land a starring role in the movie? You've never even taken acting lessons."

"Steven says I have natural talent. That's why he cast me opposite Dirk."

My mouth dropped open, stunned. Aunt Amber had never acted or performed in public that I was aware of. "You bewitched him, didn't you?"

Aunt Amber didn't answer.

"You know it doesn't count unless it happens naturally."

"It is natural. Steven spotted my natural abilities." Aunt Amber sniffed and turned away, indicating the discussion was over.

I froze as I spotted Dirk Diamond headed in our direction. His brown hair had grayed at the temples, and he was shorter than I expected, but still incredibly handsome. He wore a western shirt, cowboy boots, and jeans.

A woman walked beside him in two-inch pumps. Her trendy flowered dress was covered with a white linen blazer buttoned at the waist. Her brunette hair was pinned up in a loose bun. She wasn't in costume so I assumed she wasn't part of the cast. "That's him! That's—"

"Dirk Diamond," Aunt Amber finished my sentence. "He's my co-star. That woman with him is his agent, Kim Antonelli."

"I don't believe it." I've always thought of movie stars as ordinary people, and it amused me to see people acting silly in front of their big screen idols. Yet here I was, star-struck. Dirk Diamond had a real presence about him, even off the screen. I felt drawn to him like a magnet.

I grinned like an idiot, speechless.

"Hi there." He winked and smiled at me before turning to Aunt Amber. "See you in a bit, Amber." He waved and walked past us to Scarabelli's trailer.

"Dirk Diamond just winked at me!" The whole idea of Aunt Amber co-starring with a mega star like Dirk Diamond defied logic. "You used magic. Somehow you've bewitched the entire cast and crew into thinking you're a star."

"Of course I'm a star." Aunt Amber pouted. "Are you doubting my abilities?"

"How exactly did you get 'discovered'?" I made air quotes with my hands. There had to be more to the story. There always was with a witch involved.

"Steven and I go way back. He always told me I should go into acting, that I had charisma." Aunt Amber shrugged. "He lost his female lead at the eleventh hour. Friends help friends out. It really doesn't matter how it all came together, just that I'm part of it."

I was skeptical of her version of events. "Why now after all these years? You've never been interested in acting."

"Steven was in a pickle when Rose suddenly died. I'm just helping him out. It would have taken forever for them to hold new auditions and then negotiate a new contract. Steven can't afford any delays or new talent. He's way over budget on the film already. So I stepped in."

"Rose? Rose who?"

"Rose Lamont."

I gasped. "Dirk Diamond's wife? When did this happen?" I hadn't heard about it on the news, and Dirk hardly looked grief-stricken. On the other hand, he was an actor, so he knew how to mask his emotions. I turned around just in time to see him enter Steven's trailer.

"About a week ago. Rose Lamont had a brain aneurysm. Dirk has kept it very quiet. It hasn't even come out in the news yet." Aunt Amber said. "Just thirty-seven years old. What a shame."

"Dirk doesn't seem too upset about it," I said. "I'm surprised the filming wasn't postponed if she just died." I was troubled that the location change to Westwick Corners had been very last minute too. Was there a connection? Whatever it was, the timing seemed suspect. One star was dead and the other star, the spouse no less, carrying on business as usual.

"Dirk, brave soul, has decided to soldier on," Aunt Amber said. "After a bit of a pep talk from me, of course."

"Were you there when it happened?" Rose Lamont was young, athletic, and the picture of health. Aneurysms were rare but they happened to apparently healthy people all the time. Still, the timing seemed suspicious, and I had to be certain that Aunt Amber had no involvement, even indirectly.

"Of course not! Cen, are you insinuating that I did something sinister to land this role? I'm completely insulted." She shook her head. "I was in London and I have witnesses to prove it."

Shouts erupted from Steven's trailer before I could answer.

I spun around.

Steven and Dirk's voices carried across the lot as they stood just inside the trailer. They were arguing about the contract. Kim stood outside the trailer. She cringed each time Dirk's voice rose.

I frowned. "If she's his agent, shouldn't she be inside the trailer negotiating with him?"

Aunt Amber didn't answer.

Dirk bounded down the steps and turned to Kim. "Let's go."

Kim followed for a few feet then suddenly stopped. She turned around and locked eyes with Steven as he bounded down the trailer steps after Dirk. She held her hands out, palms outward. "I'm really sorry, Steven."

"C'mon, Kim. You've got nothing more to say to him." Dirk's face flushed in anger. "Let's go."

Kim followed Dirk like a scolded puppy, a pained expression on her face.

Steven stormed after the pair. "You can't do this to me, Dirk."

"Something's wrong," Aunt Amber whispered. "Dirk was supposed to sign that contract. I'm guessing that didn't happen."

Kim grabbed Dirk's arm and pulled him to a stop just feet away from us. "You're making a mistake, Dirk. You already gave Steven your verbal approval. You want some terms changed? Let me talk to Steven and see what I can do."

Steven Scarabelli stood a few feet away, uncertain whether to pursue the pair or return to his trailer.

"Don't tell me what to do, Kim." Dirk yanked his arm from her grasp. "Unless you want to get fired too. I'm not working for Scarabelli or anyone else. I'm starting my own company. I deserve a bigger share of the profits."

"But Steven made you a star." Kim was clearly frustrated with her client. "You know this sequel will be a box office hit just like the first one. It's easy money and you already know your lines. All you have to do is show up for a few weeks, go through the motions and get the movie done. It's a done deal."

Dirk stamped his foot. "That's a lie! Steven didn't make me or anyone a star. People give him way too much credit. It's not a done deal at all. I never signed, so I've got the right to change my mind."

"But Steven trusted you. You were fine with everything last week when we discussed the terms." Kim waved her arm at the set. "Steven went ahead in good faith based on your verbal acceptance. He invested everything he had in this film. All the cast and crew will be out of work if you don't go ahead. And Steven is already committed to paying them."

"I don't care. That's Steven's problem. That script is a piece of crap and I don't want my name associated with it." Dirk made a cell phone gesture and dismissed Kim with a wave. "Call me later."

We all stared as Dirk Diamond stormed off towards his trailer. He was nothing like the guy I idolized on screen. In fact, I intensely disliked him. He was the epitome of a demanding, cantankerous prima donna. A total jerk. But he was the box office draw and knew it. Everybody had to bend over backward and cater to his every whim. They had no choice if they wanted to keep the cameras rolling.

Kim Antonelli didn't say a word. She didn't have to. Her disgusted expression said it all.

Steven walked over to Kim. "Can't you talk some sense into him, Kim? I'll do whatever it takes to keep him happy, I promise. Time is money, and I've got all these people on set waiting for the cameras to roll. Find out what Dirk wants. Whatever it is, I'll do it."

"I'll try, Steven." Kim nodded sympathetically. "But you know how unpredictable he is."

Steven looked desperate. "That's what worries me. I've got the investors breathing down my neck and I'm late on my payments. I'll go bankrupt without this film."

"Don't do anything rash," I whispered to Aunt Amber. She wanted this gig so bad that I worried she just might conjure up another leading man.

"I'm sorry, Steven. I tried to reason with him but he won't listen," Kim said. "I feel terrible about it, but what can I do? You know I'm his agent in name only. He just does whatever he wants. I'm out money too, and I really need the paycheck right now."

A man ran towards us waving a file in his hand. It was Rick Mazure, the man who had helped me with Aunt Amber's dresses earlier. "Hey, Steven, I got those rewrites done. It took me all night, but they're finished. I think it's pretty good. Can you approve them?"

Steven dismissed him with a wave. "Not now, Rick. I don't have time to read them because Dirk has just walked off the set. Unless we can calm him down, there won't be a movie to shoot."

"Again? I don't understand." Rick's shoulders sagged in defeat. "Dirk got everything he asked for in these rewrites."

"I know. Just go ahead and hand it out. I'm sure what you've got is good so I don't need to check it. Let's just hope that Dirk comes around soon so we can start filming."

"Okay, boss." Rick took off in the same direction as Dirk.

"Maybe I can talk some sense into Dirk," Aunt Amber turned to Steven. "Let me see what I can do."

"It's worth a shot. Otherwise, I'll lose millions." Steven wiped a palm across his forehead. "Whatever you do, it can't be worse than this." He turned and walked slowly back to his trailer, his shoulders sagging like the world had just ended.

"C'mon," I grabbed Aunt Amber's arm and we headed towards the set. We soon caught up to Rick. "You must be disappointed to have done all those rewrites for nothing," I said.

Rick shrugged. "You never know what's going to happen with Dirk. He's unpredictable, but things work out eventually. I'm working with Dirk on another project—a high-octane thriller. I just finished the script for that one too. I only put up with all his demands because his name on the marquee pretty much guarantees box-office success."

We walked with Rick towards the set, where Dirk had stopped en route to his trailer to argue with one of the crew.

"At least Dirk hasn't left yet." Aunt Amber headed towards him and I followed.

Dirk turned to Rick as we approached, an expression of disdain on his face. "What do you want?"

"Have you had a chance to look at my spec script yet?" Rick waved the papers in front of Dirk. "I've got a copy right here."

"Don't bother, Rick. Your script is a piece of crap. I never got past the first few pages. Your so-called thriller just put me to sleep."

Rick's face was a blank. "I'm open to suggestions. Just tell me which parts—"

Dirk waved his hand back and forth, palm outwards. "The whole thing is garbage. Don't waste my time. I've had it with all of you people. I'm starting my own production company, with my own scripts. No more parasites getting rich off my talent."

Kim materialized beside Dirk, a pained look on her face. As his agent, she got a percentage of everything Dirk Diamond earned, but judging from her expression, the trade-offs were enormous.

"Dirk, we need to talk." Aunt Amber smiled. "You can do this in your sleep. Remember what I told you about professionalism."

Dirk's scowl morphed into a meek smile. "You're right as usual, Amber. I wish I was more like you."

My mouth dropped open. Aunt Amber held some sort of spell over Dirk, only this time no magic was involved. If it had been a spell, I would have felt it. But there was no magnetic pull, no feeling of anything other than force of personality. Which Aunt Amber naturally had. Still, it was a little hard to believe.

Kim sighed, relieved that someone had reined in her boss from hell.

"Dirk is my protégé. We go way back, don't we, Dirk?" Aunt Amber turned to me. "I helped Dirk get his first big break in show business. As a matter of fact, his very first film was with Steven Scarabelli. We've know each other a very long time."

"Yes," said Dirk. "We've got history together."

"Steven needs us this time." Aunt Amber patted Dirk's arm. "Now go see Steven and get everything worked out. You'll be glad you did."

Dirk pursed his lips and thought for a moment. "Okay, Amber. C'mon, Kim."

Kim followed behind him as he reversed course and headed back in the direction of Steven's office trailer.

I studied my aunt, stunned at the hold she apparently had on Dirk. He listened to her when he would listen to no one else.

She caught my eye and smirked. "What?"

"Nothing." She wanted praise, but I wasn't dishing any out. I didn't want to inflate her ego any more than it was already.

"Don't you have work to do?" Aunt Amber tapped her foot as she stared at me.

"Huh? Oh yes, I do." I didn't think my newspaper stories were even on Aunt Amber's radar.

"My dresses aren't going to iron themselves."

"Uh...I'll get right on it." I had no intention of taking care of her wardrobe, but the last thing I wanted was another on-set tug-of-war. I had no idea where Aunt Amber's chameleon-like mood changes were coming from, but my normally even-keeled aunt was getting to be almost as bad as Dirk.

Or as bad as Aunt Pearl. I realized that I still hadn't asked her about Aunt Pearl's job.

"Good. I've got to get on set." Aunt Amber dismissed me with a wave of her hand and spun around. She crossed the street to the old bank.

I was relieved to see no sign of Dirk or Kim. They must be already talking with Steven in his trailer. I hung back and waited for Aunt Amber to enter the building. Then I turned back towards Steven's trailer, hoping to eavesdrop. Once Dirk and Kim left, I hoped to grab a few minutes with Steven for a story.

I didn't get far before I heard voices coming from the side of the bank building. I couldn't see them, but I recognized Dirk Diamond's voice, and he was talking to Steven Scarabelli. I inched closer as their voices grew louder.

"We can change the script, the terms, whatever you like," Steven said.

"Okay, fine. I want these things changed in the script."

Papers rustled and someone kicked at the dirt.

"No problem," Steven said. "Thanks a lot, Dirk. I'm really glad we could work this out."

"Oh, and one more thing," Dirk said.

"Name it."

"Fire the old lady. Either Amber West goes, or I do."

I gasped. Aunt Amber wasn't going to like that one bit.

CHAPTER 5

High Noon Heist was starting to look more like a high noon ransom. I stood across the street and watched the set crews work frantically to accommodate the changes detailed in the script rewrites. I had never been behind the scenes on a movie set before. The frenzied activity that I had earlier mistaken for chaos was actually a finely tuned symphony of cast and crew. They moved back and forth, simultaneously performing hundreds of tasks to ready the set for the first scene. And probably a hundred unnecessary ones, all due to Dirk Diamond's arrogance and unreasonable demands.

I hadn't expected the script rewrites to be more than changes to the actors' lines, but Dirk had actually demanded that the bank be painted a different shade of blue! Paint fumes wafted through the air as the painters cleaned up and dismantled their scaffolding.

I had renewed respect for the crew, forced to cater to the whims of a spoiled movie star. Despite Dirk's last-minute rewrite demands, the set was at last ready to go. All that was left were a few last-minute script updates from Rick Mazure, mostly minor continuity changes stemming from Dirk's latest set and script changes. Fortunately, they only involved a change in Dirk Diamond's lines. The rest of the bank robbery escape scene remained unchanged.

I glanced around and was surprised to see Aunt Pearl standing a few feet away. I was glad she hadn't talked to Aunt Amber yet because they might bicker and delay the filming even more. It wasn't clear whether Aunt Pearl had a change of heart or had just come to watch the action. Either way, it was good. Once the cameras rolled, she would see how interesting the props assistant job could be.

Everyone seemed relaxed and happy now, eager to get underway. Except for Dirk, who looked like he'd rather be anywhere than on set. Dirk's impatience grew by the minute, and I just hoped he didn't storm off the set before Rick reappeared with the final rewrites.

It still surprised me that Dirk had gone ahead with the movie shoot given his wife's sudden death. Could it be that he was more dedicated to the movie than to mourning his wife? Given his tirade at Steven's trailer, I doubted that. Rose Lamont had been both his wife and co-star. He was either very stoic or…something else that was too horrifying to think about.

On the other hand, I watched too many crime shows, so I always assumed the worst. Foul play was a distinct possibility, especially because Rose was decades younger than Dirk and a fitness buff. You just didn't expect people like that to expire suddenly. I made a mental note to find out more details about her sudden passing.

Stranger still was my pension-collecting aunt as Rose Lamont's replacement. The two weren't even close in age or experience, and I doubted that Aunt Amber had the same box office appeal as a thirty-something woman. And armed with the knowledge that Dirk wanted her fired, I expected the worst was yet to come.

Oddly enough, Aunt Amber didn't appear to even be in the opening scene. She stood a few feet away, posing for photographs. She had hired her own photographer to get pictures for her acting portfolio. Either she had been written out with one of the last-minute script rewrites or she had exaggerated her starring role. My hunch told me it was the latter.

"Turn a little to the left." The photographer adjusted his camera. "Yes, that's nice. Hold it right there."

"Make sure you get lots of my good side." Aunt Amber grinned at the camera. She already had dozens of shots of her good side, bad side, and off side. She also had stills with Dirk, Arianne, and a few other reluctant cast members who had grown increasingly annoyed with her distractions. So many in fact, that Steven had scolded her for holding up production.

"Here are the rewrites." Rick Mazure strode hurriedly onto the set, breathless and disheveled. His suit jacket was wrinkled, his shirt unbuttoned, and a fine sheen of sweat coated his forehead. "Pretty major changes, so check your lines, everyone." He handed each member of the cast and crew a copy of the script from a big stack of blue pages.

The heavyset, bald man beside me swore under his breath. Bill Kazinsky looked exactly like Aunt Pearl's description, but he hardly seemed lazy. Despite his cursing and complaining, he single-handedly adjusted the props for each one of Dirk Diamond's demands without delay.

"I thought they were minor." Bill snatched the last copy from Rick's grasp and scanned the pages. He jabbed his forefinger on the script. "What the hell is this? It's supposed to be knives, not guns. How am I supposed to deal with this?"

"Is that such a big deal?" I asked.

"Yeah, it's huge deal." He swore under his breath. "I'm hundreds of miles away from the studio and all my bloody props are wrong. Why can't they just get it right in the first place?"

Rick held out his hands, palms outward. "Sorry, Bill. I just rewrote it the way I was told. If you've got questions, talk to Steven. He's the boss."

From what I had seen so far, I doubted that. Dirk Diamond ran the show.

"Yeah, right." Bill cursed under his breath and stomped off to an area a few feet away. Props and equipment were stacked five feet high in a semi-circle with a small opening only a few feet wide. The stacked equipment was a fortress, configured to allow only one point of entry and protect everything inside.

I followed behind him and stopped just outside Bill's prop circle. The mini-Stonehenge allowed only one person entry at a time. Bill turned sideways and slid in through the opening. He scanned his inventory with a frustrated expression.

"Now where am I going to find five early twentieth-century guns? They don't exactly grow on trees, you know." The obese man sat down on a stool inside the fortress and rubbed his forehead.

"You need guns? I've got guns." Aunt Pearl materialized beside me. She brandished a pistol in each hand. "I can get more in a jiffy."

I mouthed a silent *no*. This wasn't the time or place to show off her witchcraft or imply she had an inside track with arms dealers. A weaponized Aunt Pearl scared the daylights out of me. Guns were much worse than fire.

"Uh...let me see those." Bill emerged from his cave and grabbed one of the guns. He turned it over in his hand. "This might actually work. We need six of them, though."

"Not a problem, wait a sec." Aunt Pearl disappeared around a corner, only to return in less than a minute with a tote bag on her arm. It was so heavy her shoulder sagged. She handed the bag to Bill. "Try these."

I was pleased that Aunt Pearl seemed interested in the props job again.

Bill took a gun from the bag. "Hey, these look really old. Where did you get them?"

"Not important, as long as you like them." Aunt Pearl fake-curtsied and batted her eyelashes. "At your service, Mr. Bill."

I turned to Bill. "Don't you have to test the guns first to make sure they work?" Aunt Pearl's sickly sweet demeanor meant she was up to something. I suspected it was a way to undermine Aunt Amber. Witch sibling rivalry was the worst kind.

"Oh yeah, you're right. Except there's not enough time to do that."

Bill frowned. "Now that I think of it, I've got some handguns that might work. Why can't Rick just write the scene properly in the first place?" Bill glared in Rick's direction. The screenwriter was either out of earshot or was purposely ignoring him.

Bill knelt down and peered into a large box. "Damn, I don't have them in my prop box. I'll have to run back to the trailer to get them."

Aunt Pearl held up her hand. "I'll go find them—just tell me where they are."

Bill shook his head. "They're locked up somewhere safe." He pointed at Aunt Pearl. "You—watch the box. Don't let anyone take anything." He turned on his heels and left.

Aunt Pearl swore under her breath. "I do all the work and get no respect. I got him his guns. Yet instead of doing something productive, I'm stuck here babysitting this stupid box of toys. They don't pay me enough for this."

"You just started. You haven't actually done anything yet. Besides, nobody's paying you anything. You volunteered to help with the props, remember?" It was pretty clear Bill didn't really need her help.

"Yeah, well. I expected a lot more excitement from an action movie. I'm really starting to regret this. I just might have to stir up a little trouble of my own." Aunt Pearl rubbed her chin, deep in thought.

A shiver ran through me. A thinking Aunt Pearl was a very dangerous thing.

"Don't you dare conjure up more guns. People might get the wrong idea." Nobody would ever mistake Aunt Pearl for a terrorist, but people would freak out if she was armed to the teeth with half-a-dozen handguns.

"I could save everyone a lot of time. Bill isn't exactly fast on his feet. There's a lot of high-paid talent just standing around." She crossed her arms and tapped her foot. "I offer to help, but he won't take it. He obviously feels threatened by me."

"I doubt that," I said. "He's been doing this for many years. He might be slow but he knows what he's doing."

Aunt Pearl shook her head slowly. "If he had read the script, he'd know that the latest script rewrite added explosives."

"How do you know that?"

Aunt Pearl rolled her eyes and pulled a sheaf of papers from her back pocket. "Let's see…right here, on page three." She tapped the page with her forefinger.

"Where did you get that?" I leaned closer to get a better look. The footer at the bottom said version five, which was one version newer than the copy Rick had just given Bill.

"Rick gave it to me." She snatched the script away and held it above her head. "It's an advance copy."

"You're sure you read it right?" Her smug smile told me she was lying. About the script, the explosives or both, I wasn't sure. What I was absolutely sure about was that her involvement had been a huge mistake.

"Of course I'm sure. Rick gave me the script as a precaution because he knows how disorganized and incompetent Bill is. Maybe I'll go and see Steven Scarabelli myself. He'll probably hire me on the spot as head of props and pyrotechnics. I can do a much better job."

I couldn't imagine pyrotechnics in a Western, until I remembered that they had dynamite back then. I shuddered as I imagined Dirk Diamond blowing up a bank safe and the old bank building collapsing into a heap of bricks. I had a feeling that any dynamite provided by Aunt Pearl would be real. The building was far too old to withstand such an event, and we couldn't afford the repairs. I hoped Aunt Pearl was lying, but I couldn't take it on faith. I had to find Rick Mazure to confirm her claim.

Or Aunt Amber. She was probably the only one who could reign in her sister's ruthless quest for power.

Aunt Amber.

I glanced to where she had been posing for photographs but she was gone. Only the photographer remained, fiddling with his equipment.

I scanned the set for Aunt Amber and spotted her at the opposite end, talking—or rather shouting—with Steven Scarabelli. Judging by her tear-streaked face, the news was out. Steven had succumbed to Dirk Diamond's demands and had fired her.

I fought the urge to rush over and hug my aunt. Knowing that I knew would only humiliate her further. I debated telling her about the conversation between Dirk and Steven, but what good would that do? Nothing I said or did would change the outcome.

I also didn't want to jeopardize the movie even further. The cast and crew brought money to Westwick Corners. Our family Inn was fully booked, and Mom was earning catering revenue too. It would be a disaster for all of us if Steven Scarabelli left town to film somewhere else. That is, if any actual filming ever got underway.

"You're going to regret this!" Aunt Amber spun around and stormed off the set, headed in the direction of her trailer. She almost collided with Bill, who had just returned with a wooden case. She cursed and elbowed past him.

Bill swore and stepped out of her way. He strode towards the cast members on set. He placed his wooden case on the ground and unlocked it before pulling out guns and distributing them to each of the actors one by one. Then he snapped the case shut and walked towards us. He held the wooden case above the large box he had been looking in earlier. Then he dropped it on top of the larger box with a thud.

The photographer's head jerked up, startled by the noise. He frowned when he spotted Aunt Amber off set.

"Cen? You listening?" Aunt Pearl tugged on my arm, apparently unaware of Aunt Amber's firing.

"Huh?" I nodded, though I hadn't heard a word Aunt Pearl had said. Luckily I was saved by the director's call. I watched the actors take their places and made a mental note to check in on Aunt Amber once the scene was shot.

Filming was underway at last.

"Places, everyone." Steven Scarabelli had returned to the set, flushed and breathless. He waved a hand towards the set, desperation now replaced with optimism.

"That better be the last change. Watch the stuff, Pearl. I need a smoke." Bill pointed at Aunt Pearl before heading across the street.

"What's in it—?"

I clamped a hand down on my aunt's bony shoulder and held a finger to my lips.

She scowled but stayed silent.

"Action!" cried Steven.

The bank doors burst open and Dirk Diamond bolted from the building. He ran into the street towards an idling black Ford Model T, his long black coat trailing behind him. He held a handgun in one hand and a bag of loot in the other. Another man in jeans and a suede vest followed behind, pointing his gun in a defensive arc around them as they crossed the street.

The Model T's driver jumped out of the driver's seat and stood beside the car, waving frantically at Dirk with one hand and clutching a knife with the other.

Then three men jumped from behind a building on the opposite side of the street, brandishing handguns at Dirk and the other man. The one in front opened fire, hitting Dirk's accomplice. The man dropped his gun and screamed. He staggered to the car, clutching his arm as he dove into the backseat.

Arianne Duval ran from the bank, screaming. She froze on the wooden sidewalk as she spotted the men. The knife-wielding driver jumped back in the Ford's driver's seat just as Main Street erupted into a spaghetti western gunfight. Bullets flew, horses shied, and dogs barked as they ran frantically around the melee. When the dust finally settled, five men laid motionless in the dirt.

"No!" Arianne screamed. She ran over to Dirk and knelt beside him. Then she turned to the camera and whispered, "He's gone."

"Cut! Great work everyone!" Steven's voice boomed. He gave a thumbs-up as he hurried off the set towards the trailers.

The actors stood and brushed the dust from their costumes.

Everyone except Dirk Diamond.

He never got up.

CHAPTER 6

"Dirk's been shot!" Arianne shrieked.

"Save it, Arianne. We're on a break." A tall, blond actor, one of the shooters in the scene, waved her off the set.

Aunt Pearl snorted. "Of course he's been shot. He's in a shootout, dummy. That's what's supposed to happen." She turned to me. "Nobody here knows what they're doing."

"Stop it, Aunt Pearl! This is no time to be sarcastic." Dirk wore a white cowboy shirt under his coat. From my vantage point, I saw a red circle slowly expand on his shirt. I realized in horror that the stain wasn't part of the movie. A fake shot required fake blood, but since the scene ended as soon as the shots rang out, fake blood was completely unnecessary.

Arianne had noticed it too.

My hand went to my mouth as realization set in. All the other actors except Arianne were leaving. Dirk remained motionless on the ground. He hadn't moved an inch.

"I've had it up to here." Aunt Pearl tapped her chin with the back of her hand. "You have no idea what it's like, taking orders from that incompetent buffoon. I'm asking Steven for a raise. I could do a much better job than Bill with one hand tied behind my back."

I glared at her. Luckily everyone was so distracted by Arianne's screams that they didn't hear Aunt Pearl's tantrum.

Aunt Pearl shook her head and shrugged. "I tried to help him, but he's too stubborn to see the error of his ways."

I ignored her. Dirk should have gotten up by now.

We had just witnessed a tragic accident, or, quite possibly, murder.

Arianne raced frantically back and forth between the building and the street, where Dirk's lifeless body laid on the dusty street. "Somebody help—he's not breathing!"

A split-second of silence followed as the gravity of Arianne's words set in. Then everyone rushed towards Dirk.

"Too late." One of the actors knelt down beside Dirk. "I think he's dead."

A collective gasp erupted from the twenty or so members of the cast and crew who had gathered around Dirk in a loose semi-circle. While no one looked quite as grief-stricken as Arianne, there were plenty of fearful faces. Everyone was in shock.

"He's been shot for real. That's no act." I turned to Aunt Pearl beside me, but she was gone.

I spun around and spotted her walking briskly away from the set. She was already a half-block away, having caught up to Steven. He must have left the set immediately after the scene had ended. Judging from his casual, unhurried gait, he was completely unaware of what had just happened to Dirk.

Bill ran towards me, a cigarette dangling from his mouth. He inhaled deeply, then pulled it from his mouth and ground it into the dirt with his foot. "What the hell just happened? Why is the crew just standing around?"

I shook my head. "Dirk's got a bullet in his chest. He's dead."

His eyes narrowed. "You trying to be funny or something?"

"It's no joke."

"I don't believe it. It's another script change, right?" Bill's eyes darted back and forth between Dirk's lifeless body and me.

"I'm afraid not." I watched his face for any sign of deception, but he appeared genuinely surprised.

Bill paced back and forth, his face pale. "How could this have happened? Who shot him? Where are they?"

I lowered my voice. "I don't know, but the bullet seems to have come from one of your guns."

"That's impossible," Bill said. "My guns weren't loaded, never are. They don't have bullets, only blanks."

"You sure about that?" I scanned the street where I had last seen Aunt Pearl and Steven. They were having a heated discussion about something, both seemingly oblivious to the tragedy now before us. I turned back to Bill.

"Of course I'm sure. I checked each gun myself before I handed them out. I don't even have bullets." He glared at me. "You think I had something to do with Dirk getting shot? Why the hell would I do that?"

I waved my hand in dismissal. I could think of a lot of reasons. "Nobody's accusing anyone. Just stating the facts. Dirk was shot."

Arianne walked quickly towards us. She halted abruptly in front of Bill and glared at him. "You gave us loaded guns? We could all be dead right now. How could you be so stupid?"

"Of course I didn't give you loaded guns. What do you think I am, an idiot? The guns only had blanks." Bill scratched his head. "I don't get this."

"You've got a lot of explaining to do, Bill," Arianne said. "You're the only one who touched those guns."

"We don't know that they all were loaded. Only one bullet was fired," I said. It was a moot point, one that could only be verified later, but I didn't want everybody panicking and jumping to conclusions.

Bill raised his arms, palms out. "They weren't loaded, I swear. Somebody loaded the gun after I handed it out."

"If anyone tampered with them, we would have seen them," I said.

"You gave them out just before the filming started. All eyes were on the set."

"Well, somebody did something. Maybe Pearl had something to do with it. Where is she?"

"She never touched the guns. I'm sure of that." Bill's desperate attempt to deflect blame really irritated me. I couldn't blame him for being angry, distraught, or both, but that was no excuse to make Aunt Pearl a scapegoat for his carelessness. I was thankful she hadn't heard his accusations. She could certainly take care of herself, but that was exactly what I was afraid of. I didn't want to give her any excuses to set something on fire.

His face flushed with barely contained anger. "You must have looked away for a minute."

"No, I saw her the whole time. Go ask her yourself. Maybe she saw something I didn't, though." I tilted my head in the direction she had gone. "She's across the street talking to Steven right now."

No doubt Aunt Pearl was angling to get Bill's job, but that was pointless now. Without Dirk Diamond, the movie couldn't go ahead. Bill's Prop Manager role was no longer needed either. A dead megastar meant no movie, at least not anytime soon.

Arianne trembled and sobbed into her hands. "How could this happen? One minute Dirk was running and full of life. The next minute he's dead."

The timing was troubling. First Rose Lamont, Dirk's wife and co-star, and now Dirk. While Rose had supposedly died from a brain aneurysm, it seemed too coincidental—and unusual—for a married couple in their prime to both die within a day of each other. Was Dirk's death a tragic coincidence, or did someone want both of them dead?

A loaded gun and real bullets instead of blanks implied that someone had tampered with the guns. Yet Bill insisted he had checked each one of them, and I had watched him hand out the guns. Aside from dozens of witnesses, the whole thing had been captured on film.

It would be a simple matter of reviewing the footage to identify the shooter.

Supposing it was murder, why commit the act in plain view of dozens of people? The killer was either extremely brazen or incredibly stupid. Or possibly trying to frame an innocent person.

I swallowed the lump in my throat, hoping against hope that my intuition was wrong.

CHAPTER 7

I grabbed my cell phone and punched in Sheriff Tyler Gates' number. "Come to the movie set, quick. Dirk Diamond's been shot."

Dozens of cast members stood in stunned silence, forming a wide circle around Dirk Diamond's lifeless body. Word had spread quickly amongst the crew. Everyone had drifted back to the set, silent and stunned at the enormity of what had just happened. Reality sank in that someone had shot the leading man, and in the process, dashed any hope of future paychecks. It also eliminated any chance of Westwick Corners becoming Hollywood North anytime soon.

"Already here." Tyler's voice echoed as he strode towards me and Dirk's lifeless body just a few feet away. His expression was blank except for his mouth, which was set in a thin hard line. "Amber just told me."

"Aunt Amber? I guess news travels fast." I frowned. "I thought she had already left the set."

Tyler tilted his head to a few feet away where Amber stood. "She said she was right here when it happened. She ran over to City Hall to get me."

53

I followed behind Tyler as he walked towards Dirk's body. He called the crime scene investigation unit on his cell phone. Westwick Corners was too small to have its own forensics and investigative staff, so as sheriff he had to rely upon the CSI unit in Shady Creek, an hour away. Tyler would have to manage on his own until his backup arrived.

I was relieved but confused to see Aunt Amber back on the set. "I was so busy watching the filming that I guess I didn't notice her here."

"There must have been a lot going on with the filming and every-thing," Tyler said. "Tell me what happened."

I recounted what I had seen. "There wasn't anything amiss as far as I could see. The gunfight scene followed the script, except that Dirk Diamond never got up when the filming stopped."

Bill shouldered his way in front of me to get Tyler's attention. "Just in case somebody's pointing fingers, it wasn't me. I didn't kill Dirk."

"Nobody said you did." Tyler stroked his chin thoughtfully. "Why did you think that?"

"Because somebody sabotaged one of my guns by loading it with real bullets." Bill rubbed his palm over his half-bald head with its disheveled comb-over. "I don't know how or when it happened, but I'm being framed. My guns weren't loaded."

Tyler raised his brows. "Where were you when the shooting happened?"

Bill looked sheepish. "Out having a smoke. But only after I handed out the guns. I personally checked each gun to make sure they only had blanks. Somebody must have tampered with them after that."

"Any witnesses?" Tyler pulled a notepad from his shirt pocket. "Who had access to the guns?"

Bill glanced around nervously. "Well, Pearl was helping me."

"She never handled your guns, though." I glared at Bill, furious at his repeated insinuation that Aunt Pearl was somehow involved. I was also a little annoyed that she had chosen now to disappear, leaving me to defend her.

In fact, I was so mad at Bill for throwing Aunt Pearl under the bus that I was tempted to curse him. But evening the score didn't help matters any. At any rate, I only knew white magic, so a curse was impossible. If only I knew of a truth spell that I could blanket over all the people here. Aunt Pearl would know, if in fact such a thing existed.

On the other hand, it was irresponsible to tamper with what was likely a murder investigation. I wondered who had a motive. Though just about everybody hated Dirk Diamond, he was the sole reason for their livelihood. With his death, everybody stood to lose.

At least, everybody that I knew of.

I refocused on Bill and Tyler. Their discussion became more heated with each passing moment.

"All I meant was that Pearl was helping me out in general," Bill admitted. "I checked the guns at the trailer before bringing them here on set. Go ahead and search my trailer if you want. You won't find any bullets."

"I'll do that," Tyler said. "In the meantime, don't go anywhere. I'll need a statement from you once I clear the scene." He was careful not to call it a crime scene, but judging from his expression, he had already concluded that Dirk's death was no accident.

"Uh-oh." I glanced across the street and saw Mayor Brayden Banks walking briskly towards us. He looked strangely out of place amongst the casually-dressed crew. His shoes, trouser legs, and even his dark suit jacket sported a thin sheen of beige from the dusty street.

The last thing Mayor Brayden Banks wanted was bad publicity. The second last thing he wanted was Tyler Gates' continued employment as sheriff. Tyler and I had started dating a few months after I had broken off my engagement to Brayden. In a small town you couldn't get much more awkward than that.

"Cen." Brayden nodded curtly at me before turning to Tyler. "Any leads, Sheriff?"

Brayden stood out in Westwick Corners even without the filming, but his dressed-for-success image was carefully cultivated. I should know. My former fiancé had always felt he was destined for greater things than Westwick Corners.

"I'm just getting started here," Tyler said. "The Shady Creek techs are on their way."

"Good. You'll need all the help you can get." Brayden's thinly-veiled threat wasn't lost on me or Tyler. Being Westwick Corners' mayor was simply a stepping stone on his journey to political greatness. At least that was how Brayden saw the world. Any obstacle in his way had to be quickly removed.

Brayden's gaze shifted to Dirk's lifeless body, then to the set. He waved his right arm in a sweeping motion. "I want all these cameras gone, everybody's cell phones seized. The press will be on this like flies to honey. The last thing we need is a bunch of media looking to sensationalize everything." Mayor Banks didn't want any bad publicity for Westwick Corners. Not for the town's sake, but for his own. And he would do whatever was needed to come out ahead.

Tyler seemed to take Brayden's micromanaging in stride, but I fumed inside. I was part of the press too. I didn't know which was worse: Brayden forgetting that I was a journalist or being referred to as an insect.

I really had to get over myself though. Tyler needed my help if he was to keep his job. Brayden was ready to pounce on any opportunity to fire Tyler if the investigation wasn't quickly concluded.

Brayden glanced around the set to make sure no one else was within earshot. "You've got until midnight tonight to find and arrest the killer. If you don't find him, you're fired."

CHAPTER 8

The Shady Creek crime scene techs arrived in record time to process the scene while the medical examiner examined Dirk's body. While the Shady Creek Police provided CSI assistance, the only investigative feet on the ground were Tyler's.

Murder or no murder, our small town simply didn't have the budget for more officers, whether hired or loaned from Shady Creek. Part of it was that we simply couldn't afford it, but it was mostly due to a more sinister reason. Brayden Banks was setting up Tyler for failure, and I couldn't let that happen.

I turned to Tyler. "You're not really going to seize everybody's phones like Brayden asked, are you? I know that's what he wants, but that's sure to start a revolt. If anything, that will get all the publicity he says he doesn't want. I think it will backfire."

Tyler shook his head. "It will just shine the spotlight on us. But I've got to keep him from interfering." He winked at me. "Maybe you can help me out a little?"

"I can." I never frivolously applied my magic, but if any occasion warranted it, this one did. I focused my sights on my former fiancé, thinking it wasn't often I got to use a spell twice in one day. I glanced around to make sure no one was within earshot, then refocused on Brayden.

I whispered the spell:

FOGGY MIND, *foggy numbers*
Forget your cares, just sleep and slumber
Soon you'll wake and remember nothing,
Not a care in the world, no trouble faced,
The last ten minutes, all erased.

IT WORKED on Brayden just as it had on Aunt Pearl earlier. I felt proud and guilty all at the same time as I watched Brayden leave. He sauntered slowly across the street towards City Hall, rubbing the side of his head.

"Well done, Cen."

I jumped at the sound of Aunt Pearl's voice. I hadn't noticed her and Steven walking back towards us. Judging by Steven's carefree expression, he was completely unaware of what had just happened to Dirk.

"Your lessons are paying off," she said in a low voice. "Maybe you can be a witch after all."

I grabbed her arm as she walked by. "I need to talk to you. Dirk Diamond really is dead." I pointed towards Dirk's body, which was now covered with a blanket.

Aunt Pearl spun around to face me. Her face was expressionless, so I couldn't really tell if she was joking or serious. "What on earth do people see in that Dirk Diamond? He exaggerates so much that it doesn't even look real. Even his corpse pose is lousy."

"This is no yoga class, Aunt Pearl. It is real," I said. "Dirk is really dead."

"I'm not surprised, with that attitude of his." Aunt Pearl shook her head. "This film's going to be a box-office dud."

"Wait—did I hear you right? Dirk Diamond is dead?" Steven's face flushed as he looked first at me, then Aunt Pearl. "That can't be right. We just shot a scene minutes ago."

"That's exactly when it happened. One of the guns was loaded with live ammunition." I recounted what I knew.

Steven overheard and retraced his steps. "Th-that's impossible! He can't be dead." He looked as though he was about to faint on the spot. "This changes everything."

I fought the urge to run and find Aunt Amber. What we had all just witnessed was either a horrific accident or murder. The next few minutes were critical for evidence gathering and witness accounts. That was a job for Tyler and the Shady Creek police, but I had to at least keep everyone from leaving.

Aunt Pearl looked unconcerned. She brushed past me and made a beeline towards Bill, who lingered around his boxes of props and equipment.

Tyler wasn't the only one who had his work cut out for him.

I followed her and grabbed her arm to stop her so she wouldn't harass Bill. "Have you seen Aunt Amber?" It occurred to me that I no longer knew what was real and what was magic. I knew that Aunt Amber had used magic to bring the movie to Westwick Corners. Had she gone further than that?

There was a chance, however remote, that Dirk's shooting wasn't real. But in my heart of hearts, I knew that wasn't the case. Aunt Amber always stuck to the rules and did everything by the book. At least—almost always. Though she had used magic to bring the movie to town, she hadn't interfered with fate when Steven fired her. She hadn't used magic to get her job back, and she certainly wouldn't use magic to kill someone.

Still, I had to find her. Maybe there was a way to somehow reverse this tragedy.

"Last time I saw Amber she was by the trailers," Aunt Pearl said. "I guess nobody's got a job now."

I turned my attention back to the scene. There had to be close to fifty people milling around us. The mood was somber. Though everyone was in a state of shock, nobody seemed devastated, or even all that surprised by Dirk's death. That struck me as odd, given they had all worked together for years on numerous movies.

"How can this be?" A sheen of sweat broke out on Steven Scarabelli's forehead.

"I can't believe it. He really is dead." Rick Mazure shook his head as he stared at Dirk's body. "Just like that, he's gone. What do we do, Steven?"

"We'll figure something out," Steven said, though he looked anything but convinced.

Arianne was hysterical. "What the hell just happened, Bill? Didn't you check your guns before you gave them out? That gun had a real bullet. Any one of us could have been hit."

"Can't be one of my guns," Bill said. "They only had blanks."

"I'm not sure what we'll do without Dirk." Rick stood. "I can't exactly write him out of the script. He was the star."

"There's got to be some way to fix things somehow. Maybe splice the film with some old outtakes?" Arianne turned to Bill. "You really screwed up this time, Bill. The guns came from you and no one else. How could you not know that one of guns had a real bullet? Don't you ever check them before you hand them out?"

Aunt Pearl's mouth dropped open. "Uh-oh."

I spun around to confront her. "What did you do?" What if the fatal shot had been a spell gone terribly wrong? Aunt Pearl wasn't one to admit mistakes, even for something as tragic as an accidental shooting. Witchcraft or not, Bill was likely to be fired. Aunt Pearl was no doubt angling for his job, a disaster in the making.

Except that without Dirk there was no movie, so what were the odds of Aunt Pearl getting what she wanted?

Zero.

"I don't understand any of this. I did check the guns." Bill glared at Aunt Pearl but remained silent. He seemed to be thinking the same thing I was: maybe Aunt Pearl had a momentary lapse in attention while guarding the props. Or maybe something worse, a momentary lapse in morals.

Bill broke out into a sweat, and Arianne shuffled over to a nearby chair and sat down. She cried softly, her head in her hands. Steven and Rick stood together a few feet away. Rick's back faced me, but I could tell by Steven's panicked expression that they were discussing what to do next.

The rest of the cast and crew stood a few feet away, huddled together and talking in low voices. Their voices drifted towards us, speculating about what had just happened and what would happen next.

Dirk Diamond was popular on-screen, but off-screen he apparently had more enemies than friends. Everyone present depended on Dirk for their livelihood, though, so it made no sense for anyone here to kill him. His star power was the sole reason for the movie's success. What should have been a quickly made movie sequel was suddenly at a standstill. Without Dirk, the movie probably wouldn't get made at all, making almost everyone here unlikely suspects. If someone wanted him dead, why not wait until after the movie wrapped? For one thing, it would have meant a lot fewer witnesses.

Tyler motioned to the canvas gazebo that now covered half a dozen tables near the food trailer. "I need everyone to clear the set. Sit over there under cover. Cen, make sure no one leaves. I'll get statements from all of you in a few minutes. "

I nodded, though Steven had already motioned the cast and crew to follow him. They congregated at the tables, all eyes focused back in our direction. By now most people had realized the gravity of the situation. The other men in the chase scene looked stunned, having realized that they could have been on the receiving end of the fatal shot themselves.

I remained convinced that the bullet was intended for Dirk all along. But how to prove it?

Bill remained on set. "You better not blame me for this. My guns definitely all had blanks. I double-checked each one before I handed them out, like I always do."

"What exactly are you saying, Bill? Are you saying I loaded those guns?" Aunt Pearl stood defiantly in front of Bill, hands on hips.

"It's much too early to draw conclusions." Tyler's face remained expressionless as he studied the shell casing. "Someone had a loaded gun. Either it was one of your prop guns, or a gun somebody else brought on the set. You're sure you checked each one?"

"Of course I'm sure. I don't even have any bullets." Bill waved his hand towards his props. "Go ahead and check all my stuff. The guns are in a case inside that big wooden box over there."

"I'll be doing that shortly."

Bill exhaled, visibly relieved. He looked longingly towards the food trailer, where everyone else waited. "Good. I'm going to grab a coffee."

Aunt Pearl pointed at Bill as he trudged toward the trailer. "He's really not very good at keeping track of his stuff."

Bill spun around. "I heard everything you just said. You of all people shouldn't be making accusations, Pearl."

Tyler held up his hand. "Stick around, Bill. I've got questions on the guns."

"Shoot." Aunt Pearl raised her hand. "I can answer your questions. Unlike Bill here, I was there the whole time."

"I was asking Bill. I'll get to you later." Tyler frowned, his normally calm expression replaced with frustration. He had enough on his hands without Aunt Pearl stirring up trouble.

I glared at Aunt Pearl, angry at her taunting. She hadn't been at the prop box the whole time as she claimed. I had witnessed her walking away from the set with Steven before the shots rang out. Clearly she was lying, though I couldn't pinpoint exactly when she had left.

Tyler motioned us to follow him and we headed towards Bill's work area. Tyler pointed at the wooden prop box. "It's locked. Got a key?"

I exhaled in relief. The lock at least ruled out Aunt Pearl. Unless you considered a supernatural break-in, but she had no motive to kill a star she had never met.

Bill nodded. He pulled a key ring from his front pocket and handed it to Tyler.

Tyler unlocked the box with a gloved hand. He opened the wooden prop box and peered inside. He pulled out a smaller box. It was also locked.

"Try the small gold key on the key ring," Bill said.

Tyler unlocked the box and peered inside. The inside of the case was red velvet, with six gun-shaped molds. "There are places for six guns, but only five guns here in the case."

"It was like that when I handed out the guns," Bill said. "One of my guns went missing."

"You could have mentioned that before." Tyler selected a gun from the case, turned the weapon over in his hand and studied it. He opened the chamber and looked inside. He repeated the steps with each gun. "Just like you said. These guns are all unloaded."

Bill exhaled, visibly relieved. "Somebody else brought their own gun."

"Who has a key to this box?" Tyler asked.

"Just me and Steven. His key is just a precaution, in case I lose mine." Bill nodded towards the food trailer where Steven stood with the others.

"Wouldn't surprise me if you lost your key," Aunt Pearl grumbled. "You can't seem to keep track of anything, guns or keys."

"Let's stay focused," I said. Aunt Pearl could easily sidetrack the whole investigation and we had no time for that.

Bill swore under his breath. "You were supposed to be watching everything, Pearl. It's your fault as much as it is mine."

I pulled Aunt Pearl towards me just as she opened her mouth to respond. "Now's not the time for a fight, Aunt Pearl. Let him have the last word."

She yanked her arm from mine and shook her fist at Bill. "I'm not going to the big house for that man's mistake."

"Nobody's going to jail." It was like watching an Interstate fifty-car pileup a split second before impact. Knowing disaster was about to strike and being powerless to stop it. Except that I was a witch. Maybe I wasn't so powerless after all.

CHAPTER 9

*A*ll the people moving around, touching things, made me a little uneasy. Tyler couldn't possibly control everything, even with my help. So I did what any girlfriend in a panic would do: I managed the situation.

Circumstances left me with no choice but to cast a frozen spell.

I squeezed my eyes shut and incanted the words I remembered reading in *Pearls of Wisdom*, Aunt Pearl's gigantic spell book. I deeply regretted not studying it more, and just hoped I didn't make matters worse than they already were.

My lack of confidence in my spell-casting abilities had created a few mini-disasters with spells gone wrong, mostly because of my tendency to overthink things. In fact, the only time my spells worked were in moments like these, where split-second action was needed. I simply had no time to second guess myself, though it seemed reckless to use my supernatural powers without thinking things through.

I slowly opened my eyes, anxious and hopeful all at the same time. What would happen if I misspoke a word? To my amazement, the spell worked!

Everyone including Aunt Pearl was frozen. Using witchcraft was a last resort, but I felt it was justified. I had to stop Bill and Aunt Pearl from bickering so we could refocus the investigation.

I had cast more spells in one day than I had in a year, and it wasn't even noon yet. If we didn't have such a tragedy on our hands, I might have stopped for a moment to celebrate my supernatural achievement. But there was no time for gloating, I realized in horror.

Aunt Pearl was already emerging from her spell. It hadn't been nearly as effective on her as it was on everybody else.

She rubbed her head, looking confused, like she had just woken up in a strange place. Her eyes met mine. "What the heck's going on? Did you just—"

"Put a spell on you? Yes. Sorry, but you left me with no choice." I glanced around, thankful that the other fifty or so people around us remained frozen in place. Spells worked differently on everyone, and somehow Aunt Pearl had built up a tolerance. Probably from Aunt Amber constantly practicing on her when they were growing up.

Aunt Pearl grimaced like she had just tasted something sour. "I guess you learned something from me after all."

Witchcraft without practice could have serious repercussions. A botched spell was bad enough, but worse still were the unintended consequences. Those couldn't always be undone. That's one reason I always hesitated to use my magic.

Aunt Pearl, now fully alert, clapped her hands in delight as she surveyed the landscape of people, frozen in suspended animation. "Well done, Cen! See what's possible when you apply yourself?"

"Let's get one thing straight. You need to let go of your argument with Bill, okay? Let the sheriff do his investigation and you'll be cleared. There's no need to pick fights with Bill."

"Sheriff Gates?" Aunt Pearl snorted. "He has it in for me. I'm about to be framed, so I have to defend myself."

I glanced at Tyler who remained motionless beside Bill. "This is bigger than you, Aunt Pearl. Please just cooperate for once. For the good of the town." I caught movement out of the corner of my eye. A few people had started to move, including Bill. The spell was broken.

Bill shook his head and looked around in confusion before turning to Pearl. "Oh yeah…and one more crack out of you and I'll have you removed from the set."

"Oh yeah?" Aunt Pearl stood just inches from Bill, hands defiantly resting on her bony hips.

I glared at her. "Aunt Pearl, there's no time—"

"Okay, that's it." Bill's face reddened. "You're fired. Now get outta here."

Aunt Pearl swore under her breath. "Steven hired me. You have no authority—"

"Stop it, both of you," I snapped. "Nobody's going anywhere until the sheriff says so." I felt eyes on me and realized that everyone was fully conscious again. And I had overstepped my authority.

Tyler watched us, a confused expression on his face. "Did I miss something? I thought we were talking about the guns."

I turned to him and shrugged. "We got a little sidetracked."

But Tyler wasn't listening. He placed the smaller gun box on Bill's workbench, then leaned over and reached into the prop box. "Wait a minute. There's something else here in the bottom of the box. Why wasn't this gun in the case?" He straightened, holding a gun identical to the others.

Bill frowned. "Hey, that's my missing gun. How did it get back in the box? It definitely wasn't there before."

"You sure about that?" Tyler frowned. "I'm still concerned over why you never even mentioned the missing gun the first time I asked."

"I never thought it was a big deal because everybody helps themselves to my stuff around here. I swear somebody has a copy of my keys too. My props always go missing, so a missing gun wasn't a surprise. It's impossible to do my job sometimes." Bill shook his head as he gestured for the gun. "Let me see it."

Tyler pulled it just out of reach. "You can look, but don't touch it. Don't want to destroy any evidence."

Bill dropped his hand and squinted at the gun. "That's my gun all right. It's got my engraving on the barrel. I still don't know when anyone had the opportunity to put it back in its place." He was visibly sweating and pale.

"Maybe you dropped it in the box and forgot." Tyler sniffed the barrel. "Trouble is…it's been fired recently."

Bill scratched his head. "That's not possible. I emptied out the larger box earlier today when I looked for the missing gun. There definitely weren't any guns inside, because I double-checked. It wasn't in the gun box in my trailer either, so someone must have removed it before the filming started."

"Maybe you just missed it." Tyler's eyes narrowed. "Where were you when the shots were fired?"

"Right here," Bill said. "I had just handed out the guns and dropped the case inside my prop box."

"You're positive that you didn't leave the box unattended at any time? Not even for a minute?"

"Well…only for five minutes when I stepped out for a smoke. But Pearl was right here the whole time. Right Pearl?"

Aunt Pearl nodded. "I never left the props. I definitely didn't see anyone."

Bill motioned towards the catering truck. "I gotta go talk to Steven. Come get me if you need me."

Tyler, Aunt Pearl, and I watched in silence as he walked away.

Tyler turned to Aunt Pearl. "Did you see or hear anything unusual during the filming, Pearl? Anyone on set besides the actors, or anything else?"

"No. Except for Steven hovering around the props." She frowned. "He seemed like he was waiting for me to leave or something. He acted nervous."

"What?" Tyler pulled out his notepad. "When was Steven here?"

"While they were shooting the scene." Aunt Pearl glared at me. "Cen was here too."

"I never saw Steven nearby. When I saw him he was over there." I pointed over to where Steven and Aunt Amber had stood just moments earlier. "He and Amber had argued just before the shooting."

"Were they still there when the shots rang out?" Tyler asked.

I nodded, then shook my head. "I'm not sure. I definitely saw Aunt Amber leave the set. As for Steven, I wasn't watching him the whole time. I don't remember seeing him leave until afterward, when I saw him with Aunt Pearl." I looked to my aunt beside me for confirmation. "They walked across the street."

Aunt Pearl nodded. "Right after Steven came over here to where Cen and I stood by the props."

"I don't remember that at all." I shook my head. "I only saw you standing beside me. I'm sure I would have noticed Steven nearby, but I didn't. I definitely didn't see anyone unlock or lock the box." Aunt Pearl's claim didn't jive with my recollection. Was she just mistaken, or was she purposely trying to throw Tyler off track?

Aunt Pearl seemed to read my thoughts as she pointed her forefinger at me. "You were too busy watching the scene. You must have at least seen the shooter. Or were you too busy daydreaming about that boyfriend of yours?"

A slight smile played on Tyler's lips. "Let's come back to that. Can you recreate the movie scene for me, Cen? Who was facing Dirk?"

"I don't know…everything happened so fast. There was a cloud of dust, and just too many people in the scene to really see anything," I said. "Maybe it will show up on the movie footage."

"Good idea," Tyler said. "We'll check that out."

"Aren't you going to arrest Steven?" Aunt Pearl grumbled. "Or Bill? I think they're in cahoots with each other."

Aunt Pearl had such a hate-on for Sheriff Tyler Gates that she constantly tried to trip him up. Maybe that's what she was doing now. But now wasn't the time or place. A man had just died, and his killer was on the loose.

"It's a little premature for that just yet. I'm still gathering evidence." Tyler turned to me. "What else did you see?"

I glanced towards the tables by the catering truck and noticed Steven among the crowd. He was talking with a couple of cameramen but kept glancing over at us.

I recounted what I saw. "I watched the scene, but I was distracted by Steven and Aunt Amber arguing across the set." I waved my hand in the general direction of where they had been standing. "I heard the shots, but thought nothing of it until Dirk never got up. I just assumed the gunfire was all part of the movie."

"How many shots were fired?" Tyler asked.

"I don't remember...maybe a dozen?" My face flushed, shocked that a man had died right in front of me and I couldn't recall the most basic details. "Does it matter? I mean, almost all of them were blanks."

I jumped at a soft feminine voice beside me.

"Can I go back to my trailer now?" Mascara streaked down Arianne Duval's cheeks. She trembled uncontrollably, despite the warm weather.

"I just need to ask you a few questions before you go," Tyler said. "Did you notice anything unusual about the scene?"

Arianne shook her head. "Not on set. But Bill never gave me my gun like he was supposed to. I had to come here and get it myself at the very last minute."

Tyler raised his brows. "From where?"

"The prop box." She lowered her voice. "Bill's so unreliable. He's always sneaking out to have a drink, and I was annoyed because no one was even here. I had to go fishing around in the box myself."

"The box was unlocked?" Tyler frowned.

Arianne nodded. "It often is."

Bill, who had returned seconds earlier, swore under his breath.

I glanced at Aunt Pearl, alarmed. Somebody wasn't telling the truth. "Aunt Pearl, you sure you were here the whole time?"

Aunt Pearl rolled her eyes. "Okay, so maybe I left for a minute. Bill called me from the trailer. He told me to find a saddle he had forgotten somewhere on the set."

That part must have happened before my arrival. Yet I had seen Bill handing out the guns. I turned to Arianne. "When did you get your gun?"

Arianne glared at Bill. "It was only about a minute before we started filming. I realized that everyone else had their guns but me, so I had to scramble over here and back. I guess Bill forgot mine like he usually does."

Bill shook his head.

If Arianne noticed, she didn't let on. "I grabbed the gun from the box and scrambled to get in place, then we shot the scene." Her mouth dropped open. "Did I fire the bullet that killed Dirk?"

Tyler didn't answer. Instead, he turned to Bill. "Is that true? Your prop box was unlocked?"

"If it was, it's not my fault—it's those damn script rewrites. Every time I turn around, Dirk's making changes. They're never minor changes either. Not only did he want the knife fight changed to a gun fight, but the script added a horse. Can you believe that—a horse? I had to find a 1900s-era saddle and a horse before the next scene. I can't be in two places at once. Yet I still get blamed for everything that goes wrong around here."

"Quit blaming everyone else, Bill." Ariane shook her fist at him. "All you do is props. How hard is that?"

Bill rolled his eyes. "By the time I discovered the missing gun, there was no time to do anything. I just figured nobody would notice with all the action in the scene."

Arianne scowled. "And you just assumed that I was less important than everyone else?"

Bill ignored her. "Knowing Dirk, there was probably gonna be another script change anyway. I just don't understand how the sixth gun got put back in the box without anyone noticing."

Tyler's eyes locked on mine.

He was thinking the same thing I was. Bill, Arianne, Aunt Pearl, or maybe even all three, were lying.

The movie shoot, and the financial fortune that came with it, was about to crash to a halt. And nothing could stop it but the truth.

CHAPTER 10

Tyler needed my help, whether he knew it or not. Witchcraft was almost certainly involved in at least some of the goings-on. And I worried that Aunt Pearl had somehow tampered with the guns. Unintentional or not, it had very real consequences. What if her actions had blurred the trail to the real killer?

Or worse. What if her actions had caused Dirk's death in the first place?

I glanced over at Tyler, who sat opposite one of the cameramen, a gray-haired, heavyset man in his fifties. Each interview only seemed to highlight the discrepancies about the guns. Instead of new leads, all of the testimony seemed to go right back to Bill, Aunt Pearl, and their conflicting accounts. We were no further ahead.

I strained my ears and caught snippets of conversation as the man recounted the moments before the shooting while Tyler made notes. He had completed preliminary interviews with most of the cast and crew, and only a few cast members remained to give eyewitness accounts.

The area outside the bank where Dirk had been shot was now cordoned off with yellow police tape. Arianne had been allowed to return to her trailer. Tyler's questioning and several eyewitness accounts had placed her at the scene but behind Dirk. The bullet's trajectory meant that she couldn't have possibly shot him in the chest. While no one had been completely ruled out, multiple eyewitness accounts had confirmed Arianne's on set location. The deadly bullet hadn't been fired from her gun.

Aunt Pearl's voice rose from where she stood a few feet away. "Why didn't you tell anybody about the missing gun, Bill? Makes you look suspicious if you ask my opinion. Maybe you killed Dirk and you're covering it up."

"Nobody asked you," snapped Bill.

"Well, it's high time somebody did." Aunt Pearl sniffed. "If you ask me, Sheriff Gates is wasting valuable time. You yourself told me you couldn't stand Dirk Diamond. Yet you didn't tell the sheriff that. You hiding something, Bill?"

"Oh, don't be ridiculous. I admit I hated Dirk, especially the way he tormented Steven. But killing him is like killing the golden goose. It puts us all out of work." He threw his hands up in the air. "I'm not an exception because we all hated him. But no star means no movie."

"I bet I could find some new talent. Some unknown actor who doesn't ask for the moon," Aunt Pearl said. "Though you'd have to pay him danger pay to work on this movie. Apparently actors are pretty expendable these days."

That was one thing I agreed with Aunt Pearl on. Both Rose Lamont's and Dirk Diamond's deaths were suspicious, to say the least.

Bill snorted. "This whole shoot is so unorganized. First we had the last-minute location change, and then all the script rewrites. I never mentioned the missing gun because the actors always seem to be above the law. They do whatever they want and never get in trouble. Nobody ever follows the rules around here."

It struck me that nobody had really explained why the location had changed from a Hollywood set lot to Westwick Corners. While I doubted that it factored into the murders, it was certainly easier to get away with murder in a small town.

"Changing from knives to guns seems like a major script change. Are the rewrites usually this significant?" I asked.

Bill rolled his eyes. "Dirk rewrites stuff all the time. But if I complain I get blamed. I never make a big deal about it because I've used up all my favors in this business and I can't afford to get fired. Steven is my last chance at a job. He's the only one willing to hire me."

"I can see why he's your last shot," Aunt Pearl said. "Steven's got a soft heart. Nobody else would put up with you for long. You're always sneaking off for a drink."

"I went for a smoke, okay? More remarks like that and I'll fire you. I'm only putting up with you as a favor to Steven."

Aunt Pearl snorted. "More like I'm doing you a favor. Even a drunk me is better than a sober you. I bet I could do a way better job."

It was a moot point because Aunt Amber had arranged Aunt Pearl's job through Steven. In the unlikely event that filming resumed, I figured that Aunt Pearl would lose her job too, since Aunt Amber was no longer speaking to Steven.

Bill held up his hands palms outward, as if to repel Aunt Pearl. "Don't even think about it, or I'll make sure you regret it."

"Are you threatening me?" Aunt Pearl stood defiant, hands on hips.

"Aunt Pearl, stop it."

"You better believe I'm threatening you." Bill shook his fist at Aunt Pearl. "You better go before I fire one of those guns at you."

Suddenly a ten-foot wall of flame shot up in front of us. I shielded my eyes from the blinding light as the heat seared my skin. I stumbled backward.

"What the heck—" Bill backed away from the flames. "Even worse than I thought. You're going to kill us all."

"You said 'fire'. I'm just following instructions." Aunt Pearl fluttered her eyelashes. "You should be more specific."

Bill lunged at Aunt Pearl, his face scarlet with rage.

I blocked him just in time. "Stop it, both of you, and help me put the fire out." Sweat trickled down my face from the heat. I grabbed the wooden gun box and pulled it away from the flames. "This is no time for tricks, Aunt Pearl. Your special effects and prop days are officially over."

"But I'm really good at it." She pouted.

"Put it out, now." I couldn't put out another witch's spell. I could cast one of my own, but in the heat of the moment my mind drew a blank.

"You want me to use witchcraft?"

Before I could answer, Tyler carried over one of the large water cooler bottles and dumped it on the flames. We all erupted into fits of coughing from the smoke as the fire was extinguished.

"Thanks," Bill said.

Tyler just shook his head and turned back to the man he was questioning.

Aunt Pearl was digging us into a deeper hole. I just hoped Brayden hadn't seen the flames from his City Hall office across the street. Steven Scarabelli probably regretted ever setting foot in our town and would never come back.

"Just go ahead and make my day, Bill. I don't care that you fired me," Aunt Pearl said. "I'm starting my own special effects company, and I'll make sure you'll never work in this town again."

"Fine with me." Bill snorted. "I can't wait to get out of this hick town. But before I do, I'll make sure your name is mud. No one in the movie industry will ever work with you. I guarantee it."

"Better lock your door tonight." Aunt Pearl grinned slyly. "On the other hand, don't bother. I've got a key to your room. Not that I need keys to get into anything."

"What's that supposed to mean?" Bill's face reddened. "You're the one who tampered with my props, aren't you? I knew it!"

"Aunt Pearl, stop it!" I yanked her away and whispered, "You realize you're incriminating yourself?" Taking away Aunt Pearl's housekeeping keys wasn't nearly enough to keep Bill safe at the Inn. I had to somehow sidetrack her so she forgot about her feud with him. "I need your help."

Her lower lip stuck out in a pout. "People say they want my help, but then it just turns out to be boring. Amber stuck me with Bill on purpose, just to keep me out of the way."

"That's exactly why I need you. I want you to talk to Aunt Amber and find out what sort of spells she's used for the movie." I glanced at Tyler. He wouldn't want my family's help because my aunts were a mess of trouble. But what he didn't know would land him an even bigger problem with Mayor Brayden Banks.

"Why bother? You already have the smoking gun." Aunt Pearl pointed at Bill. "We know Bill's as guilty as sin. He's too incompetent to cover his tracks and get away with murder."

Bill, who by now was out of earshot, still seemed to get the gist of our conversation. He gave Aunt Pearl the finger in return.

"It's true that Bill's a lousy liar and not very good at his job. His story is suspect, but it's more a smoldering gun than a smoking one. Leave that part to me. I need your expertise for something else. Why did Aunt Amber bring *High Noon Heist* to Westwick Corners in the first place?"

"You want me to investigate my own sister? I'm not Big Brother, you know. Or Big Sister." Aunt Pearl made air quotes with her fingers.

"You want someone else to?"

Aunt Pearl shook her head slowly as realization set in. "I doubt witchcraft got Dirk killed. But even if Amber screwed up, I know she never meant to kill anyone."

"I don't know what happened and who's to blame, but I know witchcraft is what brought the movie here. We need to separate what's real from what's contrived, otherwise the investigation could go in the wrong direction."

"You mean Sheriff Gates could go in the wrong direction." Aunt Pearl snorted. "The sheriff wouldn't see the killer in plain sight. Why should I help him?"

"Do it for me, Aunt Pearl." I squeezed her arm a little harder than necessary. "And hurry. There's no time to waste."

I just hoped it wasn't too late.

CHAPTER 11

Tyler and I watched Aunt Pearl disappear down the street in search of Aunt Amber. She had no sooner left when Brayden Banks stormed towards us, his face flushed in anger.

"Uh-oh." Tyler's eyes locked on mine. "Here comes trouble."

I nodded politely at Brayden but he studiously avoided my gaze. Our break-up had been many months ago, but it was always awkward in a small town. We constantly ran into each other no matter how hard we tried to avoid it. And there was no avoiding the fact that my new boyfriend was Brayden's subordinate. If it was hard for me, it was even worse for Tyler.

Brayden scanned the set before eyeing Tyler up and down. "Finding Dirk Diamond's killer is our top priority. Drop everything else and focus on this and nothing else. We need it solved yesterday."

"I'm on it," Tyler said.

Brayden shook his head slowly, like a father disappointed with an irresponsible son. "I don't see much happening here at all. You don't even know where to start, do you?"

"Actually, we've got a few good leads—"

"Leads?" Brayden snorted. "You should have the killer by now."

Brayden Banks' sole motivation as mayor was to make a name for himself and Westwick Corners, in that order. The murder of a big Hollywood star was just the ticket, as long as the case was solved. No doubt he would take all the credit too.

Tyler stood his ground. "The autopsy will be done tomorrow, and we've narrowed down a list of suspects."

"Do I have to do your job for you, Sheriff Gates? Scarabelli did it. Anybody can see that." Brayden's half-smile told me that, despite the circumstances, he enjoyed every minute of berating Tyler in public.

Tyler opened his mouth but thought better of it.

"Have you interrogated him yet?" Brayden tapped his foot impatiently, a thin sheen of dust coating his Italian calfskin shoes.

Tyler shook his head and spoke in a low voice, "Scarabelli's next on my list."

I felt compelled to come to Tyler's defense. "He's already found the likely murder weapon. Forensics still needs to examine it."

"Nobody asked you," Brayden snapped.

Tyler's mouth tightened into a thin line as he held his temper in check.

"Why didn't you interview Scarabelli first?" Brayden frowned. "Word on the street is that he and Diamond had contract issues. So Scarabelli kills him. Not only does he solve his problem, but he collects the insurance money too. Apparently you weren't aware of that."

"Steven Scarabelli put a price on Dirk's head? I don't believe it." I flashed back to Aunt Pearl's claim of Steven standing by the prop box. It put him at the scene—except that I hadn't seen him there, and I had been standing right beside her. Our eyewitness accounts sort of canceled each other out. Either one of us was wrong, or one of us was lying.

Brayden shook his head. "You're so naïve. Scarabelli knew Dirk was going to be difficult, maybe even back out of the film. He took out insurance policies on his main stars. He killed Dirk to collect the insurance money. Aside from not having to put up with his cantankerous star anymore, he doesn't even have to finish the film. It's his retirement fund."

I flashed back to Rose Lamont's sudden death. Maybe somebody wanted the couple dead, but Steven Scarabelli seemed an unlikely suspect. A blockbuster sequel would almost certainly make more at the box office than any insurance payout. Dirk was difficult to work with, but it was still harder for Steven to make a living without him. He couldn't film the sequel without his stars. And it was obvious to everyone that Steven loved his work. I couldn't imagine him doing anything to stop it. Everybody seemed to love him too.

Everyone but Dirk.

Someone gasped beside me. I turned to see Aunt Amber. She was arm in arm with Aunt Pearl.

"Is it true? Dirk is really dead?" Her eyes were red from crying and mascara was smeared across one cheek. "What happens to the movie?"

"Filming's on hold for the moment," Tyler said. "We've got a killer on the loose."

Aunt Amber's hand flew to her chest. "Oh my goodness, as the leading lady, I'm probably next. First Rose, and now Dirk. I'll need police protection. My life's in danger!"

Brayden rolled his eyes.

"You're safe, Amber," Tyler said. "I promise."

Brayden snorted but didn't say anything.

"You were fired, remember? You're not in the movie anymore." The words slipped out before I could stop them.

Aunt Amber's mouth dropped open. "You knew that already? Before I even did? Cen, you're worse than Steven. You, my own flesh and blood, betrayed me! I thought Steven was my friend, but he just took advantage of me."

"I'm sorry, Aunt Amber. I only overheard it just before Steven talked to you." I had inadvertently exposed her secret, and now everyone else knew she was fired too. I understood her anger, but we had no time for hurt feelings with a killer in our midst.

Brayden gave Amber a strange, confused look.

Tyler turned to Brayden. "Where did you get this information on Scarabelli?"

"I'm friends with the Los Angeles D.A.," Brayden said. "They've been investigating Scarabelli for months. He's heavily in debt and close to bankrupt. His future rested entirely on this film."

No doubt our little town would soon be swarming with Hollywood tabloid reporters willing to give Brayden the airtime he craved. And he would pass on every detail to his L.A. connections in the D.A.'s office.

"Then killing Dirk Diamond hardly makes sense," I said. "This movie would have earned Steven Scarabelli millions. Why kill the main star?" Dirk's killer was almost certainly a movie insider, but my gut told me it wasn't Steven Scarabelli. Aside from being well liked and respected, he loved movie-making. I just couldn't see Steven killing off the star that made him millions.

Aunt Amber gasped. "Steven was desperate, but he wouldn't kill anyone. Not even for money. I know he had a tight budget, but killing Dirk accomplished nothing. He would have made way more money at the box office. He just had some temporary cash flow problems."

"No wonder you got the part!" Aunt Pearl snorted. "He couldn't find anyone else at the right price and he was desperate to fill the role. I knew there had to be a catch."

"Are you doubting my talent?" Aunt Amber placed her hands on her hips.

I stepped in between my two aunts. "There's no time for fighting. Let's do what we can to help find the killer."

Aunt Pearl's brows knitted together. "First Rose Lamont and now Dirk Diamond. I'd say that Brayden's probably right. Steven Scarabelli has found a new income stream. You better watch your back, Amber. No doubt he's got an insurance policy on you too."

"That's ridiculous. Steven's a jerk, but he's not a killer. " A flicker of doubt crossed Aunt Amber's face for a split second. Then it was replaced by anger. "If he fired me, he sure as heck isn't collecting insurance on me."

"Maybe it doesn't matter whether you're in the movie or not." Aunt Pearl smirked.

"Of course it matters!" Aunt Amber's voice broke as she wiped tears from her cheek. It wasn't clear what she was more upset about—her firing or Steven's supposed motives.

"Aunt Pearl! Don't speculate about things like that. It's dangerous." I made a cutting motion across my neck. I didn't want to give Brayden even more crazy ideas.

"Scarabelli and Diamond have had a lot of run-ins lately. Word is that Diamond was about to drop Scarabelli. Some technicality in the contract or something," Brayden said. "Scarabelli was deeply in debt."

That jived with the argument I had overheard earlier, except for the contract part, since Dirk Diamond hadn't actually signed the contract yet. Apparently Brayden's source was unaware of that one detail.

"I'll look into it," Tyler promised.

"You better do more than look into it," Brayden said. "I want Scarabelli arrested by the end of the day. Otherwise I'm calling in the Washington State Police."

"We don't have grounds to arrest him," Tyler protested. "I need to do a full investigation before reaching any conclusions."

Aunt Pearl waved her hand like an overzealous first grader. "What about the prop—"

I clamped a hand over Aunt Pearl's mouth. "Never mind."

"He's a flight risk, Sheriff Gates." Brayden scowled. "Either you arrest him or I'll get your replacement to do it."

Tyler opened his mouth to reply but apparently thought better of it. There was a long silence before he spoke. "All right. I'll have the killer arrested by the end of today. You have my word."

CHAPTER 12

The Westwick Corners county jail was located on the main floor of city hall and consisted of three rooms, four if you counted the lone jail cell. I sat alone in one of the two offices adjoining the interview room. My eyes focused on the large two-way glass window that separated the office from the interview room where Tyler interviewed Steven Scarabelli. I was there both as a witness and in case he needed corroboration in court. Steven's interrogation was taped, but since the aging video equipment sometimes malfunctioned, I was his backup plan.

Unofficially I also assisted Tyler by taking notes and watching Steven's body language. True, I wasn't a police investigator, but as an investigative reporter, I was adept at noticing anomalies and "tells" that people sometimes revealed under pressure. My hunches often unearthed secrets, something I hoped would be the case today. Tyler had to solve Dirk's murder quickly if he was to escape Brayden's attempts to fire him. He had no other job prospects in town, and the last thing I wanted was a long-distance relationship.

Tyler and Steven faced each other across the table in the next room. The camera angle provided a clear view of Steven, who leaned forward with his forearms on the table. He seemed anxious to cooperate and clear up any questions. Tyler was visible in profile. He leaned back and let Steven do most of the talking.

Steven Scarabelli's voice broke as he grew increasingly frustrated. "I swear I never went near the props or the gun. Your witness is lying."

That witness was Aunt Pearl, who had conveniently made herself scarce since Steven Scarabelli's arrest. It was now just after 4 p.m. The clock ticked towards Brayden's deadline, but we were no closer to the truth.

"Okay, fine. Tell me about Dirk's contract. Why wouldn't he sign?" Tyler asked.

"I have no idea. I gave him everything he asked for and more," Steven said. "Looking back, it was almost like he knew from the start that he wasn't going to sign no matter what. He was playing a game with me. Like he was trying to exact revenge or something."

"Why would he do that?"

"Mean streak?" Steven shrugged, then slumped against the chair back, as if retreating from his troubles. "I feel bad saying that about someone who just died, but it's the truth. I have no idea why he was being difficult. I got Dirk started in this business, so I don't know why he'd want to hurt me."

"You're not the one who got hurt the most, though. Dirk's dead." Tyler leaned forward. "Maybe Dirk wanted out of the contract and you didn't like that."

"No—I gave him all kinds of concessions. Things I would normally never give up, like a big percentage of the box-office receipts. Things I really couldn't afford to give. But I did anyway because I had no choice. I couldn't lose my biggest star."

"Maybe in the heat of the moment you lost your temper. All his unreasonable demands..." Tyler's voice trailed off as he met Steven's gaze.

Steven held up his arms in protest. "We had our differences, but I had less of a reason to kill him than anyone. In fact, I'm bound by contract to the rest of the cast and crew to pay their full wages on a movie I can no longer make. That was the deal I made to convince people to come to this out-of-the-way town. I'm pretty much financially ruined now. Where am I going to find a star with the same box-office draw as Dirk? He was frustrating to deal with, but I never wished him dead."

I had reached two conclusions about Steven Scarabelli. One, he was exceptionally good at incriminating himself. Two, he was innocent.

I scribbled a note to check Steven's claims. The payroll for cast and crew was undoubtedly large. If Steven was telling the truth, then any insurance proceeds he got were likely to barely cover his bills at best. Insurance policies on star actors probably just made good business sense, as opposed to being part of some sinister plan.

On the other hand, Steven Scarabelli had lost his two main stars within days of each other. They just happened to be husband and wife. That seemed highly suspicious. Rose Lamont's death had been ruled as natural causes, but still…

I jumped as something crashed in the outer office. My heart sank. It was probably Brayden coming to apply more pressure.

But it wasn't Brayden.

CHAPTER 13

"Yoo-hoo…anyone in here?" Aunt Amber's artificially cheery voice drifted in from the outer office.

I swore under my breath. Just what we needed—supernatural interference from a spoiled wannabe star.

The door clicked open. "Cen! I still can't believe Dirk is dead. He was such a dear friend." She dabbed her eye with a tissue, though her eyes were dry.

I jumped from my seat and held a finger to my lips. I nodded towards the interrogation room where Tyler was just wrapping up his interview with Steven Scarabelli. "Shhh. What are you doing here?"

"I should ask you the same." Aunt Amber's eyes narrowed as she peered through the glass. "Ooh, that man! At least he's finally locked up for killing Dirk. I've come to provide my eyewitness account so we can really nail him. I saw the whole thing."

"That's impossible," I said. "You were still with Steven when the shots were fired. I saw the two of you talking with my own eyes."

Aunt Amber didn't answer. Her gaze was riveted on the two men on the other side of the glass. She waved at Tyler, then shook her fist at Steven Scarabelli.

"They can't see you, Aunt Amber. It's a two-way mirror."

"Oh." Her shoulders slumped in disappointment as she reached for the door handle to the interview room.

"Stop! You can't go in there," I hissed. "They're in the middle of the interview."

Aunt Amber's hand dropped to her side and she sat down across from me. She sighed. "Since when did you become so bossy?"

I ignored her and refocused my attention on the men in the next room.

"For the last time, I didn't kill Dirk," Steven was saying. "His death has financially ruined me. I got everyone to sign their contracts and then he pulled out at the last minute. I'm committed to paying them, but I've got no movie to earn money. I can't do the sequel without Dirk, and now that he's dead, I have no way to recoup my losses."

Aunt Amber bolted from her seat. "That liar! He gets all that insurance money."

"Sit down." I waved her back to her seat. "Tyler knows all that. Just let him handle things."

Tyler inched his chair a little closer to Steven. "When he quit, he pushed you over the edge. You knew Dirk wouldn't finish the film no matter what, so you got revenge."

Tyler was awfully convincing, though I knew he was skeptical of Steven's guilt. I just hoped that Brayden's pressure for an arrest didn't force a false confession from an innocent man.

"That's insane. I wasn't anywhere near Dirk." Steven rubbed his forehead. "I was too busy carrying out Dirk's latest command, which was to fire Amber West."

"No! That's a lie!" Aunt Amber cried as she jumped up from her chair. "Dirk was my friend. Steven's the one who betrayed me."

"Quiet. Let him talk." I held a finger up to my lips. Sooner or later she was going to burst through that door, and all I could do was stall her as long as possible.

Aunt Amber glared at me and began pacing back and forth as the two men continued talking. "Steven Scarabelli is an evil, despicable man. I should put a curse on him."

I rolled my eyes. "You're overreacting, Aunt Amber. You better not steer a murder case off track just because you lost your job. Let the investigation take its course." I turned my attention back to the interrogation.

"Dirk wanted you to fire Amber?" Tyler jotted something on his notepad. "Why?"

"Dirk found Amber really annoying. He had promised her a bit part to shut her up, but then she started demanding things like her own trailer, higher placing in the credits, stuff like that. She's the sole reason we're even filming here in Westwick Corners. She sold me on free accommodations and no payments to the town."

I glared at Aunt Amber. "You know we can't afford that." The revenue from our bed and breakfast barely covered our overdue utility bill. We couldn't afford to operate without any payments at all.

"Liar." Aunt Amber spat out the word as she went for the door handle again.

I grabbed her shoulders and steered her towards my chair. I leaned against the door, deciding to stand guard to prevent any outbursts or interruptions. She would have to get through me first.

"Is that really true about the free accommodations? We're hosting all those people at our inn for nothing? And feeding them too? We can't afford to do that." Mom's last Costco bill was over three thousand dollars. Steven wasn't the only one with cash flow problems.

Aunt Amber shrugged. "What difference does it make? The movie's not going ahead."

Anger churned inside me. There was so much I wanted to say, but now wasn't the time. I refocused on the men who sat opposite us on the other side of the glass.

"Hmm." Tyler frowned. "Why would Amber make all those promises if she already had a part in the movie?"

Steven's face flushed. "You don't think Amber's firing gives her a motive to kill Dirk, do you? Because we can alibi each other. We were together the whole time."

Aunt Amber's hand flew to her mouth. "He's twisting everything around."

I shook my head. "Steven's defending you. Why are you being so critical?"

"The whole time?" Tyler scribbled something on his notepad.

"Well, most of it. She ran off just before the scene started shooting. I remember that because at first I had worried that she would run on set and disrupt the filming. So I was relieved when she left in the opposite direction."

Aunt Amber swore under her breath. "I'll bet he was. That jerk."

My heart skipped a beat. Maybe Steven Scarabelli had walked over to the props after Aunt Amber left, unnoticed because everyone was focused on the filming. I had been distracted by Aunt Amber, watching her running away. It was possible he had walked towards Aunt Pearl and me without me noticing. For the first time, I was uncertain. Maybe it wasn't so much what I had remembered, but what I wanted to believe. I refocused on the men in the next room.

Tyler frowned. "There's one thing that I just don't understand, Steven. Why would Dirk be the one deciding on film credits and who gets their own trailer? As producer, don't you determine the actors' perks? Dirk is just another actor that works for you, even if he is the star. Why would Amber ask Dirk for favors?" Tyler leaned forward in his chair. "He's not running the show. You are."

Steven sighed. "She figured I would say no. In fact, I had already said no to some of Amber's more outrageous demands. Then she went to Dirk and complained about me. She knows that Dirk has—had—a lot of leverage and he routinely stops production unless his demands are met. I think she went to him out of spite."

"Is that true?" I whispered.

Aunt Amber shrugged, her eyes fixated on the two-way mirror. Her face was flushed with barely contained anger.

"When exactly did he ask to have her fired?" Tyler asked.

Aunt Amber's strong personality meant she was difficult sometimes, but I never thought she was manipulative. It surprised me that she would go to Dirk after Steven had nixed her requests. I had always thought she was above that sort of behavior. Maybe the promise of stardom had gone to her head.

"Just before shooting started," Steven said. "Her complaints really set him off. Dirk told me that either she goes or he did. He wasn't going to even finish the scene with her there."

I flashed back to the argument outside Steven's trailer.

"I thought Dirk had already pulled out of the film." Tyler seemed to read my mind. He scratched his chin and scribbled a few sentences on his notepad.

Steven sighed. "He pulled out of the next film, not this one. The first bit of filming here in Westwick Corners was just to wrap up some outside location scenes. The movie was almost done."

Now I understood why Aunt Amber wasn't in the scene. Her movie hadn't even started filming yet.

"Amber was fired from the next film then, just before filming on that one starts?" Tyler asked.

"That's right. She took it pretty hard." Steven shook his head sadly. "I wish Dirk hadn't insisted because I could have handled it differently, made it a lot easier on her. Amber only had a couple of scenes, a minor speaking role. Now she hates me, and it breaks my heart. Amber and I have been friends for decades. It sickens me to think that she thinks I'm the one that wanted her gone."

I turned to Aunt Amber. "Is that true?" Her claim of starring in a blockbuster was apparently a gross exaggeration by Steven's account. His version made a lot more sense, since my aunt's starring role had struck me as odd in the first place.

She just scowled at me, arms crossed. A solitary tear ran down her cheek as she turned away.

It still seemed unlikely that Steven had killed Dirk, except for Aunt Pearl's account. But was she telling the truth? There was no corroborating evidence to substantiate her claims. At least not yet.

Steven shook his head. "Amber's scenes probably would have ended up on the cutting room floor, knowing Dirk. I thought that firing her was such an extreme measure."

"That evil man!" Aunt Amber shook her fist at the two-way mirror. "He's making up this elaborate lie to cover up what he did. I'm not letting him get away with this!"

"Let the sheriff do his job, Aunt Amber." I grabbed my aunt's shoulder but it was too late.

She already had her hand on the doorknob to the interview room. She swung open the door and burst in. She pointed her forefinger at Steven Scarabelli. "That's your killer. I saw everything!"

CHAPTER 14

It took the better part of an hour to calm Aunt Amber, but she eventually saw reason. Getting fired seemed inconsequential now with the filming halted. No one ever had to know because the movie would probably never get made. Her firing would never be made public and she would never lose face.

Now that Aunt Amber understood the gravity of the situation, she had at least backed off accusing Steven of murder. My eyewitness account of her leaving the scene before the shooting started corroborated Steven's. All of that meant that she couldn't have possibly witnessed Dirk's murder.

So why had she lied?

That a grudge or at best, a faulty memory, could result in a murder charge was disturbing, to say the least. It was doubly disturbing to hear those claims from my honest-to-a-fault aunt. I guess she was so wrapped up in this movie thing that she wasn't her usual logical, reasonable self. That aside, we weren't any closer to making headway in the investigation. The side leads just wasted everybody's time and efforts. It was almost certain that Steven Scarabelli was not Dirk's killer. In the meantime, the real killer remained free and able to strike again.

The only good thing to happen in the last few hours was Mom bringing us dinner. She had even convinced Aunt Amber to head back to the Inn to relax for a while. That brought a smile to my face. I knew Mom would quickly put her to work. Not necessarily a bad thing.

I sat across from Tyler in his office. Our half-finished plates of Mom's barbecue chicken had grown cold as we scanned through the movie footage, frame by frame, in slow motion. Even on the large fifty-inch screen, it was hard to see all the action. The multiple shooters and dusty street obscured so much that we couldn't tell who was firing at any given time. Even then, five of the six guns shot blanks, so it didn't really enlighten us much. The trick was to figure out which gun fired the deadly bullet. Since Dirk was the star, the camera focused on him. That made it easy to see exactly when he was shot, but harder to determine who the off-screen shooter was.

"Maybe one of the cameras shot a different vantage point?" I was hopeful.

"Not according to the cameramen, and we've reviewed all their footage."

"I never thought this would be so difficult," I said. "Not that many crimes are filmed. Yet even with all the witnesses and actual film footage, we still can't see what happened."

Tyler nodded. "Since the blanks were all fired at the same time as the bullet, it's almost impossible to figure out who shot him. All we can do is rule out everyone except those on the left side of the set, based on the angle of the shot. The problem, though, is how to determine who stood off-camera on the left. With no camera footage, we can only figure that out by process of elimination."

He froze the screen and pointed at Dirk with his pencil. "See Dirk's facial expression? He's in pain. This is right when he got shot."

I grimaced. "It's morbid to capture a person's death like this." I had hoped the footage could identify the killer, but the cameras mostly focused on Dirk as the star. Since it was an action scene, the background was out of focus for much of the time, so that didn't help either.

"Everybody seems to be out of position to shoot Dirk," Tyler said. "A bullet from one of the actors' guns would have hit him in the back, since they were chasing him. Yet he was shot in the chest."

"True," I said. Dirk's male costars were directly behind him, with Arianne trailing a few feet in the rear. Everyone watching the filming on set was behind Dirk too. "The footage rules out every actor in the scene, and almost all of the crew working nearby."

While the film footage didn't incriminate anybody, at least it ruled out the actors and some of the crew. It still didn't clear Steven Scarabelli. In fact, it strengthened the case against him. Or at least it would in Brayden's eyes.

Then there was the murder weapon. How it got to be in the bottom of the prop box remained a mystery, at least to me. But Aunt Amber's accusations coupled with Aunt Pearl's eyewitness account of Steven's prop box tampering had left Tyler with no choice but to arrest Steven. That made Brayden happy, but it troubled me.

Despite Aunt Pearl's claims, we had no verifiable evidence placing Steven at the scene. Even if he had been near the prop box as Aunt Pearl claimed, that would have occurred after the chase scene where Dirk was shot. Prior to that, he had been talking with Aunt Amber at the same side of the set as the actors, which gave him an impossible angle to shoot Dirk Diamond in the chest.

Tyler tilted his head towards the lone jail cell where Steven was locked up. "You're sure you saw him with Amber?"

I nodded.

"If that's true, then he couldn't have shot Dirk," Tyler said. "I've got an innocent man behind bars and my hands are tied. Unless I find the real killer, I can't release Steven. If I do, I'll be out of a job, and Brayden will probably call in the National Guard or something."

"We can't let that happen." I stabbed a piece of cold barbecue chicken with my fork. "How long can you hold him for?" I just hoped it was enough time to track down the real killer.

"I have to either release him or charge him within twenty-four hours. It's bad enough that he's locked up, but to charge him? The bad publicity will ruin him and I refuse to do that."

"Either way you lose," I agreed.

"At best, he'll be trashed in the tabloids. At worst, he'll be convicted at trial and spend the rest of his life in jail. While the real killer remains free. All because of your overzealous ex-boyfriend."

Over-jealous was more like it. I was convinced that at least part of Brayden's behavior was revenge for me dating Tyler. There wasn't much I could do about it, but it was frustrating all the same. I threw my hands up in the air. "It's not my fault."

"Sorry, Cen. I'm not blaming you. It's just hard investigating a murder with a crazy boss breathing down my neck. One slip-up and I'm out of a job."

"You know, you could always apply for a job with the Shady Creek Police. We'd only be an hour apart." I just couldn't see any way out of this. Brayden had it in for Tyler no matter what.

"No, Cen," Tyler said. "I won't let Brayden intimidate me. He'll just replace me with someone who says yes to everything. Justice is already hard enough in a small town."

"I guess he won't be mayor forever." It seemed like forever, though, and I hated the almost constant pressure Brayden applied and his urge to close the case at all costs. I couldn't let political pressure result in locking up an innocent man, even if I had to resort to witchcraft to do it. Interference felt wrong too, but at least it was less wrong.

Tyler sighed. "It sure feels like forever."

"I know. I'm also sure that Steven didn't do it. I saw him arguing with Aunt Amber with my own eyes. I just don't understand why Aunt Pearl saw something different." Eyewitness accounts often varied dramatically because memories were often unreliable. But left unproven, my eyewitness account—one that could clear an innocent man—was practically worthless. My testimony was basically canceled out by Aunt Pearl's.

"I know that too," Tyler said. "Steven killing his biggest star ends his own movie career too. From what I understand, he's pretty much bankrupt, and this movie would have put him in the black again. But if Steven didn't kill Dirk, then who did?"

"Let's look at your list again." I walked over to Tyler's whiteboard where he had made a list of the cast and crew. I studied the names, all of whom had already been interviewed on at least a cursory basis. I placed checkmarks beside each person whose location had been independently verified by the film footage or, in the case of the camera operators, by the camera angles and witnesses.

There were still dozens of people present that couldn't be eliminated, though. There were set crew on standby and at least a few dozen locals watching the filming. People free to kill if they could get away with it. Bill and Pearl were just two examples. Each person had to be alibied by others present. Their stories and credibility had to be vetted as well.

"I got nothing." I sat down, dejected at our lack of progress.

"Let's try watching again." Tyler started the film again, advancing to the moment of impact. He paused the film and tapped on the screen. "Watch the left side of the set. That's where the bullet came from."

Dirk clutched his chest a split second before his eyes darted to the opposite end of the street as if locking his gaze on his killer. A flash of recognition crossed his face at the exact moment he fell to the dusty street.

Dirk had seen his killer.

I followed Dirk's gaze but there was no one there. Just empty buildings, their dark windows contrasting against their bright, freshly painted exteriors. I walked closer to the screen and squinted at the large screen, trying to see behind the windows.

But they revealed nothing. Whatever secrets the dark windows held would stay there, shielding a killer on the loose.

CHAPTER 15

My face was inches from the screen as I squinted, still looking for shadows in the pixels.

But there was no one, not even a shadow. Dirk's killer might as well have been invisible. He or she was well hidden, despite being on a movie set with multiple cameras and dozens of witnesses.

It gave new meaning to murder in broad daylight.

I stepped back from the screen as Tyler paced back and forth in the darkened office. We had watched the footage for hours but were no closer to identifying the killer.

While the scene's brightly lit street made it impossible to see anyone inside the buildings, the most puzzling of all was the bullet's angle. Based on the trajectory, the shooter must have hung out an open window or door, at least temporarily revealing their location. Yet there were no signs of open doors, and none of the storefront windows actually opened. There were no broken windowpanes either. Unless the shooter was invisible, I just couldn't figure it out.

"Maybe the killer left a clue behind. We should check inside all the buildings," I said.

"I've got an idea." Tyler held up a forefinger as he stood in the doorway. He turned and headed to the jail cell. "Back in a minute."

I watched the door close behind him and grabbed the remote to rewind the footage.

"Yoo-hoo!" A high-pitched voice drifted down from the ceiling.

I looked upwards, surprised to see Grandma Vi's ghostly apparition floating near the ceiling.

I jumped up from my chair, alarmed. "What are you doing here?" Grandma Vi hardly ever left home, and I had no idea why she was here.

"I guess you forgot," she sniffled, on the verge of tears.

I didn't think ghosts could cry, but I felt myself getting teary eyed too. "Of course I remembered." I couldn't for the life of me remember what I was supposed to do. Dirk's death had blocked out everything else.

"Then why didn't you come home? We were supposed to make love potions, remember?"

My hand flew to my mouth. "Oh, Grandma, I'm so sorry. I guess I lost track of time. I promise I'll make it up to you." I felt a twinge of guilt as I realized how worried she had been. Grandma Vi never left home because she was always afraid of getting lost. Ghosts couldn't exactly flag down passersby for help. Yet she had left the sanctuary of home and taken a grave personal risk over concern for my welfare.

And I had totally forgotten about her.

"Tomorrow?" I smiled hopefully as she floated down to eye level.

"You're never home anymore, Cen. It's like you have no time for your Grandma anymore. Everybody always forgets about me." She shook her head sadly. "I guess I'm the one who needs a potion pick-me-up. Nobody wants me anymore."

"That's just not true, Grandma. I just lost track of time, that's all." I instinctively leaned into her for a hug, forgetting she was a ghost. I crashed down on the table. "Ouch!"

"Saw that one coming."

"Tyler urgently needs my help with a case." I debated revealing the details but just as quickly changed my mind. There was already too much West family interference, and Grandma Vi's ghostly antics would just take things up to a whole new level.

"Even more reason, Cen. You let work come between you two and before you know it, you're strangers."

"It's just temporary. I was planning to come and tell you, but I got delayed." I felt terrible lying, but I'd feel worse hurting Grandma Vi's feelings by admitting I had forgotten. The truth was that I couldn't possibly leave Tyler at a time when his job and our future were in jeopardy.

"You and Tyler are so bor-ring. You're like an old married couple. You need the potion, Cen. Love Potion Fourteen, I think. Hmmm… maybe Number Twelve. You don't realize it, but you're in dire straits. Let's get your love life back on track before it's too late."

"Um…sure, Grandma. I promise I'll be home in a couple of hours, and then we'll make our potions." She was part of the reason we were a boring couple. Tyler couldn't see or hear Grandma Vi, but having her as a roommate meant endless guilt whenever he stayed overnight. She was respectful of our privacy, but just knowing she was there made me uneasy. And while Tyler knew of my supernatural talents, he had no idea that my ghostly grandma always hovered in the background. It wasn't even something I could explain because the whole ghost thing defied logic. Even to people who believed in witches.

Grandma Vi shook her head. "You want to keep that boyfriend of yours, you better spice things up. Just look at you two, watching the same movie over and over in a boardroom. That's not how a man courted a woman in my day. Where's the romance?"

"It's not a date, Grandma. We're working." Admittedly part of the reason I stayed late with Tyler was because it was the only time I had alone with him. Things were even more crowded than usual with Aunt Amber rooming with us while she was in town. With the two of them, my secluded treehouse refuge seemed more like an Airbnb. "There's been a murder."

"Oh, I know all about the murder, Cen. I saw the whole thing."

"You were there? But you never go out." My mouth dropped open.

"Of course I was there! I wouldn't miss my daughter's movie debut for anything." Her transparent form darkened like a 1970's mood ring. "I was so looking forward to seeing her scene, but then that guy got shot. I guess the dead guy means Amber's Hollywood Walk of Fame star will get delayed."

"Aunt Amber got fired, Grandma. She won't be in the movie after all. Didn't you see her talking to Steven Scarabelli?"

"No. I was watching the scene, waiting for her to appear. Only she never did."

That gave me an idea. "Were you floating above everyone, just like you are now?"

"Yes, why?"

"Because there was someone there that wasn't supposed to be."

"I was wondering about that because I couldn't figure out that extra person." She hovered by the projection screen.

"Who?" I barely got the words out when a loud clang reverberated through the building. It was the sound of metal on metal, the cell door hitting against the cell walls. "Hurry up, before Tyler comes back."

"Cen, listen carefully. I saw something from my unique vantage point. Know who pulled the trigger?"

"Who?" I craned my neck to follow her as she floated upwards toward the ceiling.

She raised her arms for dramatic effect. "It wasn't one of the actors. It was—"

Tyler burst into the room, followed by Steven Scarabelli. Tyler looked puzzled as he scanned the room. "Is someone else here?"

"No." I shook my head. "Just talking to myself."

Tyler frowned and turned to Steven. He motioned him to the chair I had been sitting in moments earlier. "Never mind. I'm releasing Steven for now. He's given me his word that he won't leave his room at the Inn, at least until tomorrow."

"Uh-huh." Grandma Vi mouthed something but I couldn't read her lips.

"Huh?" I strained to hear.

"Cen?" Tyler frowned. "Why are you staring up at the ceiling?"

"What?" I jerked my head down. "Uh, sore neck. Just stretching."

Tyler pulled a swath of papers from his desk and placed them in front of Steven. He tapped the papers. "I'm releasing you with the promise that you don't leave town. Sign here at the bottom."

Steven did as he was told, scrawling an illegible signature at the bottom of the page.

Tyler unlocked his side desk drawer and pulled out a clear plastic bag with a wallet, keys, and the rest of Steven's personal effects. He handed them to Steven. "There's a driver waiting outside to take you directly to the Inn. You're to go straight to your room. Don't leave it except for meals in the dining room. No matter what, don't leave the property and don't leave town. Understood?"

Steven nodded. "Understood."

"Good. Because otherwise, I'll have to arrest you for murder. You won't get bail either."

"I'll stay in my room," Steven said. "I've got lots of calls to make, so that'll keep me busy."

"I suggest you make one of those calls to a lawyer, and quick," Tyler said. "This isn't over yet."

I waited in the room while Tyler escorted Steven to the waiting car outside.

"Can we go now, Cen? I haven't got all day, you know." Grandma Vi darted back and forth in front of the open door, clearly impatient.

"Soon, Grandma, I promise." I finished talking just as the outer office door clicked open.

Tyler didn't hear me this time. He returned to the inner office and sat down, exhausted.

"What if Brayden finds out you released Steven? He'll be really upset." Tyler's plan seemed like a huge gamble to me. I didn't want him to lose his job over releasing Steven Scarabelli.

"I'll deal with that when the time comes," Tyler said. "As long as Scarabelli cooperates, Brayden won't be the wiser. I realize it's a little unorthodox, but Steven's not our killer. His room at the Inn is a lot nicer than a jail cell, and I'm confident we can get your Mom and Pearl to keep tabs on him."

"That's a great idea," I said, though I wasn't entirely convinced. Aunt Pearl would love the idea of being involved, but the trouble was that she always got too involved. On the other hand, if it kept her occupied, she would stay out of other trouble. Maybe I could even convince Grandma Vi to keep tabs on Aunt Pearl.

Tyler nodded. "It frees me up too, since Scarabelli will get his meals at the Inn. That way I don't have to worry about him. I'll have more time to investigate. It's better for Steven too. Rumors are starting to circulate that he's a suspect. Out of sight, out of mind."

"Ooh, I get to guard a criminal!" Grandma Vi rubbed her ghostly hands together with glee.

"He's not a criminal," I hissed at the ceiling. "Nothing's been proven."

"Will he be handcuffed? Do I get a gun?" Grandma floated two inches from my face.

"No handcuffs." I shook my head. "Definitely not a gun." Ghosts couldn't carry weapons, much less pull a trigger. It wasn't her I was worried about. A gun could definitely fall into the wrong hands. Which was why we were here in the first place.

"Why are you talking to yourself, Cen?" Tyler's brows knitted together as he frowned. "You've been acting so weird lately. I think you're losing your mind."

"I'm just tired. Thinking out loud helps me focus." I glared at Grandma Vi, hoping she would take the hint and disappear back home, but she didn't budge. I had no plans to introduce my ghost grandma, invisible or not. Grandma Vi used that to full advantage.

"Focus pocus." Grandma Vi laughed and winked at me. "Nothing a potion won't cure."

If only things were that easy.

CHAPTER 16

$\mathcal{I}$ left Tyler at the Sheriff's office and headed to the Westwick Corners Inn to see if Mom needed any help. As I walked up the driveway to the Inn, I heard voices and laughter coming from The Witching Post, the bar and grill my family operated on the grounds. It was less than a hundred feet from the Inn, so I made a last-minute detour to see what was happening. I wasn't surprised that some of the cast and crew would be drowning their sorrows with alcohol, and The Witching Post was about the only place in town to do it.

My suspicions were confirmed as I opened the heavy wooden door and entered the bar. The Witching Post was abuzz, filled with cast and crew. Those staying in Shady Creek had obviously opted to stay in town and let off some steam. Aside from mixed feelings about Dirk Diamond himself, it seemed that everyone was waiting to see if there were any new developments in the case.

Given everybody's generally inebriated state, the mood was more like a Friday night payday than mourning. The bar resembled a library scene in an Agatha Christie whodunit, except that everyone was drunk. Their alcohol-fueled guesses and speculation were rampant, with everyone taking turns guessing who had killed Dirk. Some claimed Dirk had mob connections, and others suggested it was a love triangle that got him killed.

A few even thought that Dirk's death was just a well-executed publicity stunt and expected him to burst through the doors of The Witching Post at any moment, angry as ever.

Yet one thing was crystal clear. Not one person in the bar thought that Steven Scarabelli had killed Dirk. There was even a half-hearted attempt to chip in funds to get Steven a lawyer, though it didn't get much traction now that they were all unemployed. That's how well liked Steven was.

I spotted Aunt Amber in a corner booth and slid into the bench seat opposite her. "Feeling better?"

"I did everything to help Steven and look where it got me." Aunt Amber scooped the last of the peanuts from the dish in the center of the table and dropped them in her mouth. "My career is ruined."

I grew alarmed as she grabbed another bowl of peanuts from the adjacent table. Aunt Amber ate when she was upset, but at the moment, she seemed out of her mind and oblivious to everything around her, including the peanuts that she tossed back with reckless abandon. Giant welts formed on her arms and neck, making me wonder if she had a death wish. "Stop eating those. You know you're allergic."

"I can't live like this, Cen." Aunt Amber cried. "What about my Hollywood Walk of Fame? Now I'll never get there."

At least the corner booth we sat in gave us some privacy, but even in the bar's dim light, Aunt Amber's bloated face was clearly visible. "Just calm down and take a deep breath. Where's your EpiPen?"

"Oh, darn it." She lowered her head and rubbed her face in her hands. She recited a spell in a low voice, so softly that I couldn't make out the words. Within seconds her hives shrank by half.

I breathed a sigh of relief that she hadn't placed a curse on Steven or anybody else. I grabbed the peanut bowl and took it over to the next booth.

I slid back into my seat. "Did you use witchcraft to get the movie part in the first place?" There were strict rules about using witchcraft for personal gain, and Aunt Amber knew them all by heart. She was normally so law-abiding and the last person I expected to break the rules. But nothing about this day had been normal.

She ignored me as she stared into space.

I grabbed her hand and squeezed it. "Aunt Amber?"

"There, I feel better now." She looked up, her eyes meeting mine. Her skin was clear and pale, with no trace of the hives from moments earlier. "All this stuff is stressing me out. It's all my fault. I should never have helped Steven."

"You helped him how? I thought it was the other way around." I couldn't see how else Aunt Amber had landed a blockbuster movie acting role with absolutely no experience or acting credits.

"Of course I helped him, Cen. I got him Dirk Diamond."

I rolled my eyes. "How can you say that? Steven already had Dirk Diamond. *High Noon Heist* is the sequel to *Midnight Heist*, which Dirk already starred in. It was a blockbuster hit, so naturally he's going to star in the sequel."

"You would think so, but Dirk hadn't signed the contract yet. For good reason too. He thought Steven was giving him a bum deal."

"How do you know what Dirk Diamond thought?" I lowered my voice as I spotted Steven Scarabelli enter the bar. I swore under my breath, alarmed to see him out of his room. I just hoped that Brayden didn't decide to stop by the bar.

I turned back to Aunt Amber. "Dirk sounded pretty ungrateful when we were at Steven's trailer. Yet if not for Steven, Dirk wouldn't have even been a star." It felt weird to talk about Dirk in past tense, though I couldn't shake the image of his dead body. It was seared into my brain.

A flash of light caught my eye. I turned to see flames shooting up from behind the bar.

Aunt Pearl waved at us from behind the bar. She was either doing a poor job bartending or a good job of burning the place down.

I jumped from the booth, cursing as I hit my knee on the table. I ran towards the bar, slipping on the wet floor as I went. I regained my balance. "Aunt Pearl, grab some water! Douse the flames!"

She grabbed a bottle from the bar and waved it in her hand.

As I ran towards her, I noted in horror that it wasn't water, but a bottle of vodka. "No!"

I dove to grab the bottle before everything exploded, but I hit an invisible wall with such force that it had to be supernatural. I tumbled to the ground and bounced into a backward somersault before unrolling into a sitting position.

I turned around, expecting an inferno. Instead, the flames were now contained in two tiny shot glasses like the whole thing had never happened.

Everyone in the bar stared at me for a split second, then someone clapped.

Aunt Pearl smirked. "C'mon, Cen. Pick yourself up."

I glared at her as I staggered to my feet. "Drawing attention isn't going to get you a career in the movies, Aunt Pearl. Stop the theatrics."

"Oh, like you should talk. Relax, Cendrine. You act like you've never seen flaming Sambucas before." She lifted the two drinks with her oven mitt-covered hands and placed them in front of Steven Scarabelli and Arianne Duval.

I was a little uneasy about Steven hanging around at the bar. Though he had broken his promise to Tyler to stay in his room, at least he was still on the property. There was nowhere else to go at this hour, and odds were slim that Brayden would visit the bar. It would probably be fine.

Steven and Arianne both looked stressed, and it was certainly understandable why they wanted drinks after everything that had happened today. Especially Steven, who was probably still shaken from spending time in jail. Even though people weren't exactly mourning Dirk, flaming Sambuca shooters seemed a little too cele-bratory for my liking. I wondered whose idea that was.

Arianne shrank back from her shooter and fanned her hand above her shot glass. "Can I get mine uh…cooled?" She nodded politely in my direction.

Aunt Pearl rolled her eyes before leaning over to blow out the flames on Arianne's drink, almost singeing her own eyebrows in the process.

Arianne shuddered and pushed away her shot glass with a long manicured finger.

Thankfully Steven changed the subject. "Have you seen Bill?"

"No." It seemed odd for him to ask me, of all people. "Did you check his room?"

He nodded. "I was there a few minutes ago, but that jerk is avoiding me. He owes me money and I can't wait any longer. I'm on the hook to pay everyone here."

"How much does he owe you exactly?" The money angle interested me because money always seemed to bring out the worst in people. Bill hadn't mentioned any issues with Steven. Maybe Bill was embarrassed about owing money. But admitting that Steven was there to collect a debt from Bill would have been good to know. That at least gave Steven a valid reason for lingering around the props. But if that was the case, why hadn't Steven said so? Or maybe Bill just claimed Steven was at the prop box to deflect blame from himself.

I felt a hand on my arm and turned to see Aunt Amber at my side. With Steven on my other side, I felt a little uneasy about things escalating. "We should probably go help Mom now."

"Fine by me." Aunt Amber turned to Steven. "You might think you're getting away with murder, Steven, but you're not. If the police don't get you, I will."

"Aunt Amber!" I locked my arm in hers and steered her away from the bar towards the door. "How can you say such a thing to the man who gave you your big break?"

"My talent is what got me my break, Cen. And I in turn helped Dirk. Aside from being my protégé, he was a dear friend. He never forgot how I introduced him to Steven and gave him *his* big break. It turns out to have been a fatal mistake. It's all my fault." She broke out in sobs as I guided her to the door. "Maybe I should just end it all. Without my co-star, I have no reason to live."

I pulled open the door and half-dragged Aunt Amber as she leaned heavily on my arm. I couldn't tell if she was serious or just trying to get attention, but I suspected the latter. She wanted Steven to regret the loss of her amazing acting skills.

As we stepped outside into the cool night air she suddenly regained her strength. She dropped my arm and headed for the Inn at a brisk pace. We had only walked a few steps when we ran into Tyler coming from the parking lot.

"You." Aunt Amber lunged at Tyler and pounded on his chest. "You let a murderer go free. You gave him his freedom, but I promise you, he's not going to enjoy it."

CHAPTER 17

I had just entered the dining room when something swooped down and almost knocked me off my feet.

I screamed.

I ducked as a swoosh of air hit the back of my neck. I froze, half-expecting claws on my head or back. While the Inn was drafty, there were definitely no bats, birds, or flying creatures inside the house. No, this could be only one person, and that's what scared me more than anything. I froze by the stair banister, bracing myself for what was to come next.

"Cendrine West—stop cowering like a fool!" Grandma Vi hovered in front of me, blocking my way forward. In theory at least, since technically I could walk right through her.

"What are you doing here? I thought you went back home," I whispered. Grandma had promised to go back to the treehouse, but I guess she was upset at all the guests staying at the Inn. She was never happy about people staying in her ancestral home, and I worried about her doing something rash. Just her presence was enough to complicate things.

I felt eyes on me. Despite the late hour, the dining room's two dozen or so seats were occupied with late diners, and all eyes were on me. Grandma Vi was invisible to everyone else, of course, so I just looked like a raving lunatic.

Again.

"Let's go somewhere else," I said. "Maybe the treehouse?"

Grandma Vi's apparition darkened. "This is my house, remember? I've got more right to be here than these interlopers. This is all Amber's fault. None of this would have happened if she hadn't brought that movie here. I'm a little cheesed off at her."

I spun around to look for Aunt Amber, but she hadn't followed me into the dining room like I thought. I turned on my heels and headed to the hall. "I'll find her."

Grandma Vi floated behind me, muttering something I couldn't quite make out. Her voice rose as we moved to the hallway. "You're supposed to be helping poor Tyler. He's really got his hands full with this one. And he looks so sad."

Tyler did look sad. We passed him where he sat at a table by the door. It was getting closer to Brayden's deadline, and he was no closer to catching the killer.

Grandma Vi was Tyler's biggest fan, but her man crush on my boyfriend was a little annoying sometimes. And kind of stalker-ish. He didn't even know she existed, yet she knew everything about him. I had this disturbing family secret that if revealed would only make me seem creepy too. "I am helping, Grandma, and I don't want to argue. Let's focus on finding Dirk's killer. You said you saw the whole thing. I want to know what you saw from your vantage point above the set. Tell me everything."

She floated past me and turned around, hovering at my eye level. "There were some other people on set that weren't supposed to be there. No one saw them but me."

"Who?" I momentarily forgot about my search for Aunt Amber.

She shook her head. "A man and a woman. I don't know who they are, though. They were hiding in an empty building across the street."

Of course. As a ghost, Grandma Vi not only passed through walls; she could see through them too. Why hadn't I thought of that before?

"Which building? Could you identify—" I stopped mid-sentence as the Inn's front door creaked open. Brayden Banks stepped inside the dining room seconds later. He nodded, his voice flat and cold. "Cen."

No one would ever guess that we had once been madly in love and engaged to be married. As far as he was concerned, I was now the enemy.

His mouth was set in a thin, hard line and it was obvious that he was angry about something. I debated stepping in front of him to warn Tyler, but it was too late. He was already headed towards the dining room.

So I fell in behind him and motioned for Grandma Vi to follow.

Brayden strode into the dining room and made a beeline for Tyler, who had just been joined by Steven Scarabelli at his tiny table. Steven must have left the Witching Post just after Aunt Amber and me. Tyler leaned forward, talking with Steven in hushed tones.

Brayden stopped inches from Tyler and glared down at him. "Sheriff Gates—is this your idea of crime fighting? Sitting around drinking coffee with a murder suspect?"

Tyler stood. "That's not what I'm doing. I'm getting eyewit—"

"Sure you are," Brayden said in the flat monotone he used when trying to control his temper. "Just relax and drink your coffee. That way the State Police will know exactly where to find you when they absolve you of your duties and take over the case."

"You can't take me off the case. Not when I'm getting close to an arrest."

"Just watch me," Brayden said. "You were supposed to have Scarabelli behind bars. What the hell's going on here?"

"I couldn't arrest him. There's conflicting evidence that says we arrested the wrong person." Tyler tapped his laptop screen. "He's promised not to leave the Inn."

Brayden threw up his hands and his face flushed with anger. "How could you release Scarabelli? We can't have a murderer on the loose. What will people think?" It was all about appearances with Brayden.

"Uh, I'm not going anywhere, Mayor," Steven said. "I'll stay right here."

Brayden dismissed him with a wave. "Keep out of this."

Steven shrugged. "I'll be upstairs in my room, Sheriff." He turned and left.

Tyler pressed a few keys on his keyboard and swiveled his laptop around so it faced Brayden. "I had no choice but to release Steven. Look what I found."

It was surveillance video footage from the bank's outside cameras. The film was black and white and grainy, but Steven Scarabelli was in plain view. "He was right there when the bullets were fired. You can hear the shots. You can also see there's nothing in his hands. He's standing in the opposite direction from where the bullets came from."

"I don't care." Brayden's face reddened.

I interrupted. "You don't care if an innocent man is charged with murder? I thought I knew you better than that, Brayden."

Brayden shook his head. "You don't know me at all, Cen. You never did."

Grandma Vi hummed and played a fake violin. "What drama!"

I glared at her before turning back to Brayden.

Bullets weren't the only thing flying around Westwick Corners. "Let's focus on finding the killer, who's still out there," I said. "Until we figure that out, we could end up with another murder on our hands."

"Stay out of it, Cen. It's a police investigation and none of your business." Brayden suddenly jumped backward as he clutched his head.

The ceiling above his head had cracked, sending chunks of plaster raining down. A fine dusting of plaster coated his head and the shoulders of his navy suit. Directly above him was a gaping hole in the ceiling. The hole had opened for no apparent reason and had only hit Brayden and not the rest of us.

Grandma Vi floated just behind Brayden, laughing.

I was mad and pleased with her all at the same time, and it was all I could do to suppress a smile.

"This place is a dump." Brayden rubbed his face in his hands, brushing the dust from his eyes. Maybe it was the plaster shower or the threat of a killer on the loose, but something had a sobering effect on him. The worsening situation seemed to hit home for Brayden. "I'll give you twenty-four more hours, Sheriff Gates. But after that, I'm calling in the State Police."

"You won't have to. We'll have the killer before then." Tyler frowned.

I just hoped he was right. We had to stop the carnage before the killer did it for us.

CHAPTER 18

After checking in with Mom in the kitchen, Tyler and I headed back into the dining room. Aunt Amber had reappeared. She sat at a table just outside the kitchen door, tapping her foot. She looked flushed and restless. Probably because Mayor Brayden Banks was still there.

Brayden had dusted off the fallen plaster and was polishing off a double helping of Mom's cherry pie. He seemed content, at least until he spotted us heading towards his table. Aunt Amber rose from her seat and fell in behind us.

Whatever conversation took place between Brayden and Tyler, I felt that Tyler needed witnesses. The three of us stood there waiting for Brayden to look up, but he just stared down at his half-eaten pie, completely in another world.

"I did it," Aunt Amber said, loud enough for everyone in the dining room to hear. "I killed Dirk Diamond."

Brayden's mouth dropped open, his fork poised in midair. "What are you saying? You helped Scarabelli?"

Aunt Amber was quickly getting herself into a mess of trouble, too serious for even a witch to undo.

"You couldn't have done it." I stared at my aunt, willing her to stop talking. "I saw you walking away before the shots were fired."

"Maybe I never fired the actual shot, but I helped all the same." Aunt Amber smiled as if she had just uttered the most inconsequential thing in the world.

Brayden dropped his fork. "How exactly? Did you get Scarabelli the gun?"

Aunt Amber just smiled.

"You hired an assassin?" Brayden's face scrunched up in confusion.

I leaned closer and whispered in my aunt's ear. "Why are you doing this? You're just complicating things. It will sidetrack the entire investigation."

"Relax." She said in a low voice. "It's all part of my master plan."

"Forget the master plan." I gripped her arm and pulled her a few feet away. I had had enough of Aunt Amber's drama. The town—not to mention Dirk—would have been better off if the movie never happened in the first place. "This is serious business. Once you're arrested, you won't be able to go back to London."

"Uh-oh. I hadn't thought of that." She smoothed her hair and smiled at the couple sitting at the next table.

Just as I suspected, Aunt Amber was angling for the limelight without thinking things through.

Brayden pointed at Tyler. "You heard her, Sheriff Gates. Why aren't you arresting her?"

Tyler opened his mouth to answer but thought better of it. He pulled a pair of handcuffs from his jacket pocket and cuffed Aunt Amber.

"Aunt Amber! Tell him you're not serious." Her diversion tactic—if that's what it was—threatened to derail Tyler's investigation once again.

She ignored me as she held up her wrists. "I'm Steven's accomplice. We both killed Dirk."

"Lock her up, Gates." Brayden pointed at Aunt Amber. "Don't let this one get away too."

My mouth dropped open in shock at Brayden's hostility. While there was no longer any love between Brayden and me, he had actually been quite fond of Aunt Amber back when we dating. Yet now he saw nothing wrong with sending Aunt Amber to the slammer while eating Mom's pie.

"Wait! I lied—I didn't do it. But my life's in mortal danger." Aunt Amber stifled a sob as she scanned the dining room. She had a captive audience. Every single person in the dining room had stopped eating, talking and whatever else they were doing to stare at her. "I need to be in protective custody. Sheriff Gates, my life is in your hands."

For a few more minutes at least, Aunt Amber was the star attraction.

If only she knew that it came at a terrible cost.

CHAPTER 19

We finally managed to move Aunt Amber out of the limelight and into the kitchen where she couldn't create more trouble. But the damage was already done.

Grandma Vi, on surveillance duty in the dining room, had just rushed in to inform us that Brayden had just placed a call to the Washington State Police. He was looking to get them in on the investigation without Tyler requesting it.

Aunt Amber fidgeted with the handcuffs. "These cuffs are killing me, Tyler. Why do I need to wear them in the first place?"

He sighed. "You asked for them, remember? You gave me no choice but to act."

"Tyler's about to get fired because of you," I added. "Don't you feel the least bit guilty?"

"Why would I feel guilty?" Aunt Amber pouted. "I was only trying to help. You know, make it look like Tyler was making progress. Why is everyone so touchy all of a sudden?"

I shook my head. "Murder confessions can't be undone, Aunt Amber. No one's going to forget your little performance out there."

She immediately perked up. "Really? Was my acting that good? Did I convince you?"

Tyler shook his head. "This is no time for acting, Amber. I'll take the cuffs off, but you have to promise me that you'll keep your mouth shut this time. Go upstairs to your room, don't talk to anyone, and don't leave for any reason."

"But what if—"

"No exceptions." Tyler pulled me close and whispered in my ear, "I can't solve a murder and deal with your crazy family all at the same time. Can you make sure they all stay out of sight, at least until Brayden leaves?"

"I'll keep them busy." I turned to my aunt. "C'mon, Aunt Amber, let's go upstairs."

I had no idea where Aunt Pearl was. Her absence from the Inn worried me because she was likely stirring up trouble somewhere else. But I already had my hands full, so I put her out of my mind for the moment.

After escorting Aunt Amber to her room and getting her settled in with some Hollywood gossip magazines, I headed back downstairs to help Mom with kitchen cleanup. It had been an exhausting day. Morning would come early, and keeping my aunts out of the way also meant I'd have to do Aunt Pearl's housekeeping job in addition to helping Mom with everything else. We needed a plan to keep everything on track and deal with the guests.

It turned out to be good timing. Mom already had a task for me: take a room service dinner to Steven Scarabelli. Between his jail stint and drinks at the Witching Post, he had missed dinner.

I grabbed the steaming plate of roast beef, vegetables, and gravy and headed out of the kitchen. I was relieved that he finally had gone up to his room for the night. Maybe the cast and crew weren't out to get him, but Dirk Diamond's rabid fans most certainly would be seeking vengeance. It was probably a blessing in disguise that he was stuck in our little town.

In fact, in the short time since we had returned to the Inn, a half-dozen die-hard fans had shown up. I hadn't seen them with my own eyes, but according to a recently arrived crew member, Dirk's fans were camped out at the Inn's property line at the bottom of the hill. More followers were gathered around a temporary shrine of candles and flowers at the Main Street movie set.

While the fans couldn't see the happenings at the Inn as long as they stayed camped out at our front gate, they were sure to see anyone coming and going. Tyler had closed the gate as a precaution earlier, so any guests had to call for admittance. That provided a semblance of calm, at least on the surface.

Hollywood news traveled fast…really fast. No official announcements had been made about Dirk yet. Westwick Corners was remote, tucked away in Northeastern Washington State, several hours' drive from Seattle. Yet people already knew of the tragedy that had unfolded here.

I expected the town to be swarming with Dirk's followers and the Hollywood press by tomorrow morning. That gave me an idea. For once our off-the-beaten-path location gave me an edge, and I intended to use it for an exclusive interview, if I could wrangle it.

I carried Steven Scarabelli's dinner tray upstairs to his third-floor room, fully aware that for now, at least, I was the only reporter with access to him. I intended to use that to my full advantage.

My stomach growled from the aroma wafting from the roast beef sandwich and beef dip I carried upstairs. The plate was heavy with a double helping of roast beef, Yorkshire pudding, carrots, two scoops of mashed potatoes, and a separate side dish of gravy. My mouth watered as I realized that I hadn't eaten anything since morning.

I almost collided with Aunt Amber as she descended the stairs, suitcase in hand. "Aunt Amber, where are you going? You know you can't leave."

"I can't stay here, Cen. Not in the same place as a stone cold killer. What if he targets me next?"

"He's not going to do that." I balanced the tray in one hand as I held onto the banister.

"You don't know that. He betrayed Rose, Dirk, and finally me. I've had it with that man." She put down her suitcase on the carpeted floor on the landing.

As usual, Aunt Amber had somehow made it all about herself. "But Dirk's the one that wanted you fired. I was there. I heard it with my own ears."

"I wish you'd stop saying that." Aunt Amber sucked in her breath. "You're just mistaken."

"No, I'm not. Remember when you introduced me to Dirk? You headed to the set but I didn't. I saw Steven and Dirk arguing outside the old bank building. It wasn't the script they were talking about. It was you."

Aunt Amber's hands flew to her hips in indignation. "Of course it was me. Dirk was taking a stand for me. He's a very loyal colleague."

I shook my head slowly. "I'm afraid that's not the case. Dirk gave Steven an ultimatum. Unless Steven fired you, Dirk walked, right then and there. Steven protested, but in the end, he had to agree to Dirk's demands. He couldn't film the movie without Dirk. Since he had signed all the contracts, he still had to pay the cast and crew. Dirk would force him into bankruptcy. And the entire cast and crew would be out of a job. What choice did Steven have?"

"You're wrong." Amber's eyes filled with tears. "Or maybe you're just on Steven's side. He's turned everyone else against me."

"Do you really think I would lie to you, Aunt Amber?"

"I-I don't know," she sniffed. "Everybody else I trust has turned on me. I've had it with this place. I'm going back to London." She picked up her suitcase and headed down the stairs.

I sighed, frustrated. Aunt Amber was still seeing this whole tragedy from her point of view, not Steven's. "You can't leave. You promised Tyler, remember? You need his permission to leave town."

Aunt Amber was already at the bottom of the stairs. She turned her head up and glared at me. "I don't need anybody's permission. I'll do what I want, when I want."

I sighed. I didn't want Brayden to have another excuse to fire Tyler. "Please don't go, Aunt Amber. Stay for Tyler's sake. For mine."

"I just can't believe—" For the first time there was a trace of uncertainty in her voice. Her eyes flitted back and forth between the door and me.

"You want proof? Maybe I can arrange that." My magic was barely adequate to take me back to the scene of Steven and Dirk's argument, let alone bring Aunt Amber along. "We could do a rewind spell and I could show you."

"We?" Aunt Amber made quote marks with her fingers. "You've got to master magic on your own, Cen. We won't always be around to help you."

"I wasn't implying—"

"You just have to apply yourself."

"Okay, fine." I kept my voice even, trying not to betray the hurt I felt. Some way, somehow, I had to show Aunt Amber the truth. "I'll figure it out, you'll see."

Aunt Amber rolled her eyes. "I don't see how a rewind spell will help anything. I was never with you when you overheard Dirk and Steven. How can I go back to somewhere I never was at in the first place?"

A flash of inspiration hit and almost knocked me over. "Wait—I have an idea. Dirk and Steven were outside the old bank. Maybe one of the cameras filming the robbery scene was rolling and picked up their conversation." It was too much to hope for, but it was worth a shot.

That piqued Aunt Amber's interest. "If there's film, I want to see it."

"Come with me while I deliver this dinner. Then we'll go and look at the footage." Tyler wouldn't allow it, so I would have to do it without his knowledge. I felt terrible about that, but unless and until Aunt Amber dropped her accusation against Steven, the investigation was hopelessly sidetracked.

Or worse. An innocent man could be convicted of murder. "You know that Steven couldn't have killed Dirk. He wasn't anywhere near him." I recounted my observations of Steven's movements, careful not to mention anything from the murder investigation itself.

"So what? Maybe Steven used special effects to disguise where the bullet came from. I don't know how, but I'm sure he's involved somehow. Maybe he hired a hitman to do his dirty work." She pushed past me on the stairs, her elbow flattening the mountain of the mashed potatoes.

I looked down in dismay at the smeared potatoes. "Now look at what you've done."

"Really, Cen? You're worried about peaks in your mashed potatoes while we're locked up with a killer?"

I shook my head. "I can't take this food upstairs like this. It looks like somebody stuck their finger in it." Steven would assume that someone was me, and it would seriously lessen my chances of an exclusive interview. "Fix it, please."

Aunt Amber rolled her eyes. "You should be able to do that yourself, Cen. It's Magic 101, for crying out loud. You and your generation take everything for granted these days. You really need to brush up on your craft before it's too late."

I started to protest, but it was pointless to argue. Instead, I appealed to Aunt Amber's ego. "Please? You're so much more artistic than I am."

It worked. She waved her hand and voila, the potatoes were transformed back into swirly peaks again.

"There's something else—we can't find Dirk's killer without your help. You know it's not Steven. Somebody here knows something, and of all the stars…" I paused to let that last word sink in. "You're the only Hollywood outsider. You're in a unique position to help."

"I am?" Aunt Amber looked both doubtful and suspicious.

I nodded. "You're critical to solving the crime because you were so close to Dirk." And Steven, I wanted to add, but I didn't dare mention his name. I didn't want to rekindle her anger at being fired.

"I was close to Dirk and Rose too. They both looked up to me."

Aunt Amber's hand flew to her mouth as her voice broke. "Now they're both gone."

I glanced down at the roast beef, which wasn't exactly steaming anymore. I highly doubted that Aunt Amber was the catalyst for Dirk's successful acting career, but none of that really mattered anymore. There was one thing I had to know, though. "Did Rose really die from a brain aneurysm?"

"I-I don't know anymore. Both of them dying seems far too coincidental." She wiped a tear from her cheek. "She was the picture of health."

"I'm sorry to bring that up at a time like this, but I thought it seemed suspicious too." I made a note to check on the details.

"More than suspicious. It seals the case against Steven. He killed them both," Aunt Amber said. "They both trusted him and now they're both dead."

"I don't think it's him, Aunt Amber. He's financially ruined. He suffers more from their deaths than pretty much anyone. It's got to be someone else." I glanced around the hallway, afraid of someone overhearing us. Now that Aunt Amber had calmed down, she was imparting some really useful information. I wanted to keep her talking. "We really should talk in private. Come upstairs with me. I just have to deliver this plate and then we can talk."

"Okay." She ascended the stairs ahead of me, pausing on the second floor to leave her suitcase by the railing. "Where to?"

"The third floor." I purposely declined to tell her who the plate was for. If she knew it was Steven, then she wouldn't come.

She was in better spirits already. Unfortunately, it meant that her mourning had been replaced by a tirade against Steven. "Steven just flipped out over Dirk for no reason at all."

"I can see why. He had all his money tied up in the production when Dirk basically quit on him." I slowed my walk as we neared Steven's door. I didn't want him to overhear.

"There's more to it than that," Aunt Amber said. "Steven was angry with Bill too. You should ask Bill about it."

It was hard to read Aunt Amber's expression in the dimly lit hallway. "Maybe I will." I knocked softly on Steven's door, bracing myself for what was to come. I hoped that Aunt Amber would be at least civil to Steven, but maybe it was better for them just to have it out and make peace with each other.

I needn't have worried about their spat at all. A much bigger problem faced us, one that I would never have expected in a million years.

CHAPTER 20

Steven's door swung open from the pressure of my knock, sending me off balance. The dinner tray swayed precariously, but I somehow managed to right myself and steady it.

"Hello?" The door was ajar several inches and everything was eerily quiet. I felt weird just walking in, especially knowing that Steven was inside.

No answer.

"You sure you have the right room, Cen?" Aunt Amber asked.

I didn't answer, instead craning my neck around the half-open door. The lights were off, the curtains were drawn, and the room was dark except for a narrow strip of light that shone from the half-closed bathroom door. The light illuminated something on the floor a few feet inside. It looked like a pile of clothes or bedding. I pushed gently on the door but it wouldn't budge. Whatever was on the floor prevented me from opening the door.

As my eyes slowly adjusted to the darkness, I spotted a pair of feet. They were connected to the lump on the floor.

"Oh, no!" I screamed as I recoiled in horror.

"What? What's happening?" Aunt Amber pushed me forward as she tried to get a better view.

I reached inside, flipped the light switch, and recoiled in horror. The floor was covered in blood.

And Steven Scarabelli's still body.

Aunt Amber pushed me again, and this time the door pushed past Steven's feet and opened wide. The dinner tray flew from my hands and fell to the floor in a loud crash. Potatoes and roast beef spilled everywhere before the tray landed upside down on Steven's protruding legs.

I stepped back, only to collide with Aunt Amber whose face was now inches from mine. We both screamed.

"Oh, no. Not Steven." My hand flew to my mouth.

"Cen—what the heck—" Aunt Amber stumbled backward.

"Don't look." My eyes traveled from the protruding feet upwards. Steven Scarabelli's face was frozen in a grimace, a knife protruding from his chest. My mouth dropped open but no words came out. I pointed helplessly at the body.

"Don't look at what?" Aunt Amber pushed past me, only to stop dead in her tracks. "Oh, my God! Somebody help!"

I surveyed the room. Other than Steven's dead body, nothing else seemed out of order. Except for the spilled roast beef dinner which, I realized, had just contaminated the crime scene. "Aunt Amber, wait." I pointed at the blobs of mashed potatoes that coated Steven's legs. "I think I just compromised forensic evidence. This is a disaster!"

Her eyes widened as she took it all in. "It's a mess, all right. I could do a reversal spell."

I shook my head. "We can't do anything at all. It's a crime scene." I was mortified that she would even consider such a thing.

"Oh, right. I guess it is." A tear fell from Aunt Amber's cheek as she knelt down beside Steven. "We never even got the chance to patch things up. Who would do such a thing?"

I pulled her up and away from Steven's body. "We'd better get of out here before we make matters worse." I pulled out my cell phone and punched in Tyler's number.

"Steven, I found the bott—holy crap!" Bill stood in the doorway, a shocked expression on his face. "What the hell just happened?"

Aunt Amber sobbed. "Steven's dead! Cen was bringing Steven some food and…" Her words morphed into an incoherent wail as I guided her and Bill out into the hallway.

Tyler ran down the hall towards us. He pointed at Bill. "Were you with him?'

Bill shook his head. "I was just coming to his suite for a drink. I was here a few minutes ago and just went to my room to get us something else to drink." He held up a bottle of expensive-looking whisky. "I just left him a couple of minutes ago."

It had been less than a half hour since Steven had returned to his room.

"Anyone else in or out of the room?" Tyler frowned as he scanned the room for evidence of anything out of the ordinary. The bed, desk, and bathroom all appeared untouched. The only sign of occupancy was an opened suitcase beside the bureau.

"I don't think so," Bill said. "When I first came over he said he had just gotten back from a walk in the garden. He made a detour there after the bar. Said he had been thinking about the movie and replacing Dirk."

A sheaf of papers lay on the desk. As I walked closer, I realized it was a movie script. The typewritten pages were covered in red ink. Angry comments and exclamation marks were scrawled all over the pages. I bent down to study it more closely and saw that many of the comments were signed with an initial D, which I took to be Dirk.

"It's a marked-up copy of *High Noon Heist*," I said, though no one was paying me any attention.

Tyler and Bill stood near the bathroom, while Aunt Amber hovered by the door.

"I swear no one was in here when I left. And I was only gone for a minute. My room's next door, so I can't imagine why I didn't hear anything." Bill shook his head. "This is one dangerous town. What the hell's happening?"

I smelled the alcohol on Bill's breath, though I stood more than a foot away. Either he was lying or the booze had distorted his time estimate. Someone had most definitely visited the room.

"The window's open," I pointed out. The closed curtains billowed softly from the evening breeze. "Maybe the killer left down the fire escape."

Tyler walked over and pulled the curtains back. He leaned out the window to get a better view of the ground below.

I followed behind him and peered out the window. The fire escape ladder ended at the second floor. From there it was a nine or ten-foot drop to the grass below. It seemed a likely escape route. It was impossible to see from where we were on the third floor, but the killer could have left tracks in the grass or other evidence. Unless the suspect had escaped down the hallway, which implied that the killer was still inside the Inn. I shuddered involuntarily.

I lowered my voice so Bill and Aunt Amber couldn't hear. "I guess Brayden can't be mad at you now."

He sighed. "I can't charge a dead man, can I? I hope I'm not the only one crossing Steven off the suspect list."

Aunt Amber turned to Bill. "Steven was acting so weird lately, like when he yelled at you about the missing gun."

"Forget about it." Bill waved his hand in dismissal. He seemed anxious to leave.

"Wait—what's this about the missing gun?" Tyler turned away from the window to face Bill.

"I told Steven all about the missing gun as soon as I noticed it," Bill said. "He said not to worry about it. That he had bigger things to worry about."

"Why didn't you mention this earlier?" Tyler frowned. "It's an important detail."

"He's my boss—at least he was." Tears welled in Bill's eyes. "I was covering for him. I thought he'd get in trouble over the missing gun.

You know—it would look like he killed Dirk. It's kind of irrelevant now, because Steven would never harm Dirk. Or anyone."

"I'll decide what's relevant or not," Tyler said.

"It's totally important that the gun's been used in a murder." Aunt Amber's hand flew to her mouth as she turned to me. "When did Westwick Corners become such a dangerous place? I don't even recognize this town anymore."

"You should have told me, Bill." Tyler frowned. "What else are you covering up?"

"Nothing, I swear. Look, all I know is that I told him about the gun, but he said he had bigger things to worry about. What those things were, I don't know." Bill raised his hands, palms out in surrender. "I didn't want a gun to fall into the wrong hands, but when I suggested reporting it to the police, Steven said not to bother. I tried to reason with him, but he's the boss."

The only person I knew to be innocent was Steven, and now he had a knife in his chest. The man everybody loved apparently had at least one enemy.

Maybe Aunt Amber wasn't exaggerating about her own personal safety after all. As long as we were unclear on the killer's motive, everyone else in the movie was in danger too.

I shivered as I glanced at Aunt Amber sobbing into her sleeve.

Who would be next?

CHAPTER 21

Tyler called the medical examiner and the Shady Creek Crime Unit back to the Inn. Aunt Amber and I stood guard outside Steven's suite while Tyler contained the scene. The Shady Creek folks arrived in record time, and within an hour Tyler had handed off the crime scene to the ME and the forensics techs. Then we headed downstairs.

Tyler had sworn all of us including Bill to secrecy. He didn't want any details divulged until Steven's body was removed and the crime scene processed. I understood why. Everyone would freak out and immediately run upstairs. That would be pretty hard to manage since Tyler was essentially a one-man police force. With two murders, it was clear that things were escalating.

My heart sank as we reached the dining room door. Brayden was still at his table, and he immediately noticed Aunt Amber on the loose as she ran through the dining room and straight into the kitchen. She had essentially blown her chance of house arrest at the Inn, so Tyler would have no choice but to take her to the police station.

But first, he had some explaining to do before Brayden spotted the Shady Creek Forensics Van in the parking lot again. But it turned out that Brayden already had and had even been briefed by the medical examiner on her way in. Things weren't looking good for Tyler at all, and I expected the State Police to arrive at any moment.

Brayden pointed towards the kitchen door behind which Aunt Amber hid. "Get her out of here."

I wondered if Brayden thought that Aunt Amber was responsible for Steven's murder too. It seemed preposterous. But based on Aunt Amber's earlier confession that she was Steven's accomplice in Dirk's murder, maybe Brayden actually believed that Amber was a double murderer.

Tyler tilted his head in the direction of the kitchen. "I'm taking her in, but there's something I have to tell you first."

"We can talk later." Brayden seemed awfully calm, all things considered.

A little too calm, in fact. Now I was certain that the State Police were on their way. There was nothing I could do, no objections I could make, without causing more trouble for Tyler. So I retrieved Aunt Amber from the kitchen and met Tyler outside. Aunt Amber and I got in the back seat and Tyler drove down the hill, past the front gate where dozens of Dirk fans were gathered.

She unrolled her window and stuck her head out. "Help! I've been framed."

I lunged towards her, only to be yanked back in place by my seatbelt. "Stop it, Aunt Amber. You're acting like a spoiled child."

Tyler's eyes met mine in the rearview mirror. He didn't say anything.

"Acting. Yes, that's exactly what I'm doing." Aunt Amber pouted. "It's my only chance for a bit of drama."

"Well, cut it out. It's totally inappropriate at a time like this. You're worse than Aunt Pearl." My temper was frayed and I wasn't sure how much more I could put up with. I felt especially bad for Mom, taking care of everything singlehandedly at the Inn while her sisters created havoc. Aunt Pearl was probably burning down the bar right now.

We drove the rest of the way to City Hall in silence. We arrived to find all the parking blocked off by movie trucks.

Tyler swore under his breath and pulled into a parking spot a block away. I helped Aunt Amber out of the back seat and threw my jacket over her cuffs to hide them, but she flung it off and waved her cuffed hands up in the air.

"I'm innocent!" Aunt Amber wailed as she staggered down Main Street towards City Hall. "This is a travesty of justice."

Luckily Main Street was its usual deserted self. All the film people were at the Inn or elsewhere.

That didn't make me any less annoyed at Aunt Amber's theatrics. The three of us walked down the street, tired and dejected. Tyler walked on one side of Aunt Amber and I walked on the other. We headed towards Tyler's office inside City Hall.

As we got closer, something flashed. At first, I thought the half dozen or so men and women were part of the film crew, but they didn't look familiar. As we got closer I remembered that a few of Dirk's fans had gathered downtown. Except it wasn't just his fans.

There were a handful of reporters too. The news really was out, on Dirk at least. I wondered how long before they found out about Steven.

Several vans approached and suddenly there were so many rental cars and vans nearby that they created their own little mini rush hour. Based on the frantic level of activity, I feared that news of Steven's death really had been leaked. That meant either Bill or Aunt Amber. No one else really knew about it yet.

"Did you—"

Aunt Amber shushed me with a wave of her hand. "I am exerting my fifth-amendment rights, so don't ask."

"But this is important, Aunt Amber. Why are you being so difficult?"

She just ignored me. Whatever the reason, the press was now on Main Street in full force. I was shocked to see a CNN van parked across the street.

We didn't attract much notice until Aunt Amber spotted the cameras.

She screeched to a stop, almost taking me down with her. "Hey, that woman's from CNN. We're on national TV." She fake-smiled at the cameras.

I tugged on her arm. "Let's get inside. They're not interested in the movie or you, Aunt Amber. They're here because of Dirk's murder." They couldn't possibly know about Steven yet.

Aunt Amber turned to the cameras and wailed, "Help me!"

I gritted my teeth and tightened my hold on her arm, half-expecting her to bolt. "Let's just get inside."

By now a dozen or so reporters surrounded us, arms outstretched with tape recorders and microphones. "Did you kill him?"

"Hell no!" Aunt Amber yanked her arm from mine. "I did not kill Steven Scarabelli in revenge for killing Dirk."

"What? Wait!" A blonde thirty-something woman dressed for TV inched closer and stuck her recorder in front of Aunt Amber's face. "Steven Scarabelli's dead too?"

Aunt Amber turned to me, trance-like. "Can't I give an interview?"

"Absolutely not!" Tyler's mouth set in a firm line. "The only interview you're giving is to me. A murder investigation is serious stuff, Amber. Nobody talks to the media but me right now. Got it?"

"Got it." Aunt Amber looked crestfallen. "You two are quite a pair. So straight-laced and always ruining everything with your by-the-book rules. No wonder you need a love potion!"

Tyler's eyes met mine, a confused expression on his face.

"Grandma told you? Why did—never mind." I started to protest but stopped short. All eyes were on us, and anything we said or did was bound to show up in a news story. Apparently, Tyler and I were a constant news story too, at least within my family.

It seemed like an eternity, but we finally reached City Hall and stepped inside. Tyler locked the door behind us.

"I wonder if I'll be front page." Aunt Amber beamed, her cheeks flushed with excitement. She was thrilled with the media attention, even if it fueled speculation that she was a murderer.

"Stop it, Aunt Amber," I hissed. "Dirk Diamond and Steven Scarabelli are front page news, not you. Nobody even knows who you are. Nobody cares."

Her lower lip stuck out in a pout. "I don't know where you inherited your nastiness, Cendrine West. Certainly not from me."

"You're sidetracking the investigation, Aunt Amber. This is no time for acting or theatrics. If you really care, why don't you do something constructive and cooperate with his murder investigation?"

"Okay, fine," she said. "Bill wasn't the last person to see Steven alive. I was."

CHAPTER 22

It took the better part of an hour for Aunt Amber to recount her last moments with Steven Scarabelli. She claimed to be the last person to have seen Steven alive. That contradicted Bill's statement of just leaving Steven for a moment while he went next door. There was only one version of the truth, so one of them had to be lying.

Actually, they both had been caught in multiple lies, so neither of them could be considered reliable witnesses. That worried me. Aunt Amber's withholding of information was incriminating, to say the least.

After leaving the Witching Post, she had gone to the kitchen to help Mom clean up, and then left for a walk on the grounds. She claimed to have run into Steven in the gardens that surrounded the Inn. According to Aunt Amber, they had reached a truce of sorts regarding Aunt Amber's firing.

"Then I went back to the dining room. You saw me there yourself." Her smile was totally out of place.

I flashed back to her sitting just outside the kitchen, her skin flushed like a cross-country runner who had just crossed the finish line.

I knew she was lying. She had done a lot more than just saunter in from the garden. Not only that, but I doubted there was anything to negotiate about her movie role. It had gone up in smoke with Dirk's death. No Dirk meant no movie.

Tyler looked up from his notepad. "So…after the walk, Steven went upstairs and you went into the dining room."

"Uh…yes, that's what happened." Her face flushed as she dropped her gaze. "I came in through the kitchen door."

"Any witnesses?" If she had passed through the kitchen, Mom would have seen her. She was lying and I knew it.

Aunt Amber didn't answer.

Tyler frowned. "I think you were in Steven's room, whether you admit it or not. Lying just gets you in a lot more trouble. It might even land you in jail."

She shrugged as she looked around. "I am in jail."

"You know what I mean, Amber. For real." Tyler ran his fingers through his hair and sighed. "Honestly, it would be easier for me to just hand you over to the State Police. It might get Brayden off my back at the same time."

"No, you can't do that!" I hoped he was bluffing, but I couldn't really blame him if he'd had enough.

Aunt Amber started mumbling under her breath. As I leaned closer to decipher her words, I suddenly felt drowsy.

"One, two, three, make it not to be…"

I jerked my head up. "Aunt Amber, stop it! You can't use witchcraft to cover up a crime. You of all people know better." The Aunt Amber I knew was a respected, high-ranking executive in the Witches International Community Craft Association, not a cheat. The Aunt Amber I knew followed the rules. She didn't impede investigations. I was shocked at her behavior; it was like my aunt had become a stranger to me.

"I just wanted to put things back to the way they were before I disturbed them." She wiped a tear from her eye. "I'm in too deep."

My mouth dropped open. "You mean tamper with evidence? I'm shocked that you would do such a thing." Aunt Amber's surprise had seemed so genuine. I supposed her acting skills were much better than I gave her credit for.

"Why not? I know I didn't kill Steven, so I don't want Tyler to waste time investigating me."

"You were in Steven's room after he died? Why?" Tyler leaned forward in his chair.

"We never really made up during our talk in the garden, because I still thought Steven was lying. Later on, I realized it was true: Dirk made Steven fire me. I just went upstairs to apologize. But it was too late." She sobbed into her hands. "But I definitely didn't kill him."

"You were already in the room before we went up with Steven's roast beef dinner?" I flashed back to her hysterics. She really was a good actor. "Why didn't you say something?"

"I don't know. I was too scared I guess. Between that and the film edits, I guess I just thought—"

I jumped out of my seat. "What film edits? What are you talking about?"

"Well, Pearl and I thought it would be a thoughtful gesture if we went ahead and finished the movie. You know, what with Dirk gone and all... Anyway, Pearl added special effects and we edited the film a bit. Cut out the bad scenes and stuff. All we had left to do was to add my little ole scenes into the movie."

"Wait—what bad scenes?" As far as I knew Aunt Pearl didn't have any film production background.

"You know, like where an actor flubs his lines and stuff. I thought if we did a bit of cleanup it would help everybody. Pearl and I just did some of the post-production work with witchcraft so everybody would have less to do."

"And the movie would get finished faster," I said.

"Uh-huh. We were almost done when Tyler took the film." She

shook her head. "Lots of cuts. It really was a mess until we fixed things up."

"You mean the film we've been reviewing all this time isn't the original one? Did you keep a copy of the original?"

She shrugged. "Last I saw, Pearl had it. What she did with it, I don't know."

I had to get the uncut film before it was lost forever.

If it wasn't already too late.

CHAPTER 23

I searched everywhere for Aunt Pearl, but she was nowhere to be found. She wasn't downtown, at the Inn, or even at Pearl's Charm School.

I headed across the grounds to the Witching Post while Tyler discussed some follow-up details with Bill in the dining room. The voices of drunken partiers drifted towards me as I neared the bar. Judging by the noise levels, it was even busier now. Some of the locals must have drifted in to join the cast and crew.

I opened the door and scanned the bar, taking note which of the cast and crew were present. One thing immediately troubled me. Just about everyone was drunk, evidenced by their staggers, slurs and spilled drinks. Just how reliable they would be as witnesses to alibi Bill was anyone's guess.

Waiting till tomorrow seemed too late, but what choice did we have?

I spotted Kim Antonelli, Dirk's former agent, at the bar. She sat quietly, nursing an overfilled glass of red wine.

I was relieved to see Aunt Pearl tending bar. At least she was occupied, even if she was overly generous with her pours. She caught my eye and smiled. Her unusually good mood struck me as odd, but at least she hadn't shapeshifted back into her Carolyn Conroe alter ego as she was prone to do in the bar. We already had enough trouble as it was.

I walked towards the bar just as Rick Mazure, the screenwriter, sidled up to Kim. He wrapped an arm around her before giving her a drunken pat on the back. He sat down on the barstool next to hers.

"I guess you're out of a job." Rick's speech was slurred. He had obviously been drinking a lot in the last few hours.

I joined Aunt Pearl behind the bar. "Aunt Amber told me about your editing adventures. I need the original unedited film. Where is it?"

"I don't know what you're talking about." Her smile vanished as she busied herself scrubbing a nonexistent spot on the bar.

"Aunt Amber's in jail, and she's been charged with murder. Only that film can save her. Do you have it or not?" The film part was a bit of an exaggeration, but it could easily come true in a few hours.

"What's it worth to you?" Her eyes narrowed as she studied my reaction.

"This is no time for bargaining, Aunt Pearl. Do you have it or not?"

"No." She resumed scrubbing the invisible spot on the bar. "Even if I did, I'm not going to incriminate myself."

"Do you really want to see Aunt Amber go to trial for murder? Tyler can't do anything once the State Police take over. They'll be here any minute." Even Aunt Pearl had a heart. Despite her ongoing rivalry with Aunt Amber, she would never allow her sister to be falsely accused.

Her eyes met mine at the mention of State Police. She reached into her pocket and pulled out a memory stick. She pressed it into the palm of my hand. "You owe me."

"Sure," I said. "Hey, why don't you take a break? I'll take over for a while."

To my surprise, she agreed. An occupied Aunt Pearl was better than an idle one, but I wanted her away from the cast and crew in case she got any more bad ideas. I didn't want her creating more trouble for Tyler and the investigation.

I slipped the memory stick into my pocket, thinking I should grab Tyler and race back to the police station. Except I had overheard interesting little snippets of Rick and Kim's conversation, and I needed to know more.

That was the other reason I wanted to take over from Aunt Pearl—it gave me an excuse to linger. I didn't want to miss an opportunity to eavesdrop. As Dirk's agent, Kim might have some inside information on who would want to kill Dirk. Tyler had already taken Kim's statement, but maybe the wine and the bar atmosphere might loosen her lips a little.

But it was her companion doing all the talking.

"—I'm going to be rich, Kim. You with me or not?"

I busied myself arranging the bottles behind the bar. My back was to them but my ears were perked.

Kim didn't respond. I was dying to turn around to gauge her expression, but I didn't dare draw attention to myself. I had the sense that Kim either disapproved of what Rick was proposing or didn't know what the hell he was talking about. She gulped her wine and sighed.

Rick called for more drinks and I complied, delivering a new whiskey for him and another glass of wine for Kim. I stalled as long as I could in front of them by cleaning Aunt Pearl's imaginary spot on the bar.

Rick downed his glass in one shot and slammed the glass down on the bar. "I'll miss Dirk, but I won't miss his temper. He treated us all like garbage. Especially you, Kimmie." He placed his hand on Kim's.

Kim slowly extracted her hand from his grasp and placed it out of reach on her lap. "Dirk wasn't the nicest guy around, but I'll still miss him. I don't even know what I'll do without him. He was my only client, so I'm out of a job now."

"You can come work with me." Rick's hand inched closer to Kim's again. "I'm going to start my own company."

Kim shook her head. "I'm an agent, Rick. I don't write screenplays, I represent actors. I just wish I had kept more than one client, but Dirk was just so demanding. He insisted that I work for him exclusively. It paid well but look where it got me in the end. Now I'm unemployed, just like that." She snapped her fingers.

"Doesn't matter, Kim. I can make you rich. Just say the word and I'll cut you in."

"In on what exactly?"

He patted his jacket pocket. "I've got the next Oscar winner already written. All I need is for you to find me some stars to bring it to life."

CHAPTER 24

Tyler and I had reviewed the film from Aunt Pearl numerous times in the last hour. Aunt Amber had misrepresented the contents a bit. The film she had given me wasn't exactly the raw, uncut, unedited version. Instead, it was an enhanced version with bonus content.

The bonus content wasn't anything like the usual kind included with movies. Instead of funny bloopers, scene outtakes, and alternate endings, we had gotten something completely different.

"What on earth were you thinking, Aunt Amber?" My two aunts had gone completely crazy with the movie, adding explosions and other pyrotechnics every few minutes, in addition to adding a new role for Aunt Amber. Now she was the star instead of Dirk. The only *"High Noon Heist"* was the extent of the liberties my two aunts had taken with the movie.

"I can't hear you. Don't forget you've got me locked up in jail here." Her voice echoed against the walls.

"I can't believe they did this." Tyler pulled his keys from his pocket and headed into the next room. He returned in less than a minute with Aunt Amber.

Technically she was supposed to remain in the jail cell, but given the drastic edits to the film, we pretty much needed her in the interview room to give us a play-by-play. Clearly, you can't just lock up a witch and expect things to run smoothly.

"Didn't you make a copy before you made all these changes?" Tyler's face flushed, clearly frustrated at the lack of version control.

Aunt Amber shook her head slowly. "Pearl said not to bother because we didn't have time. We were just trying to salvage the film after Dirk died."

"Why would you do that?" I stared at her blankly, not understanding.

"We just wanted to finish the film so that everyone could get paid," she said. "We figured it was only short a few scenes so we made them up. The plot's a little different, but it's even better than the original in my opinion."

"Oh. My. God." I leaned back in my chair and looked up at the ceiling. I was furious with my aunts but a little touched at the same time. They just were trying to help. No—they were helping themselves.

"Don't you think so?" She smiled sweetly at us. "It's ready to be released now, so we can earn some money at the box office."

"You did this without asking anyone?" I doubted that my aunts were just being helpful and unselfish. They each wanted recognition and saw redoing the film as a perfect vehicle for self-promotion.

"I wasn't on speaking terms with Steven, remember? He's dead now, so it's not like he could give direction anyway. Nobody here seems to take any initiative, so we took it upon ourselves to save the movie. Which we did. How it happened really doesn't matter now."

"It matters a lot," I said. "The original uncut film could have helped us to identify Dirk's killer." I didn't add Steven's killer too, since I was certain that the two had to be related. Aunt Amber's take-charge personality was a serious drawback sometimes. "Now that you've altered the film, it's a lot harder to use it as evidence."

"I just wanted to help." An uncertain expression flashed across her face. "We just added our special talents—my acting and Pearl's special effects. We didn't want Bill or anyone else standing in our way, so we didn't tell anyone. It was supposed to be a surprise."

"It's a surprise all right." The extra scenes would have been comical except for the gravity of the situation. Aunt Amber had several grand entrances and crying scenes that were totally out of context for an action film, and there were at least a half dozen fires and explosions in the footage we had watched so far. And we were only halfway through the film.

Tyler paused the film and froze on the gunfight scene. "There. Look to the left. There's part of a hand there, and it doesn't belong to any of the actors."

I squinted at the screen. The image was so blurry that it was hard to tell whether the hand belonged to a man or a woman. "There's no gun, but whoever that hand belongs to is at the exact angle from where the shot came from. I wish we could see more."

I turned to Aunt Amber. "You sure you don't have an untouched original version?"

She shook her head slowly. "Sorry. I guess we got a bit carried away. I can still use the film as an audition tape, right?"

"I doubt it. I think the half-finished film belongs to Steven's estate. Not like your photographs." That gave me an idea. Aunt Amber's photographer had faced the set, directly in front of the place where the mystery hand was. "Hey—do you have any photographs from today?"

She shook her head. "I won't get them from the photographer for a couple of days."

"We need those pictures, Aunt Amber. Can you call the photographer and get him to send them to us?"

"I couldn't find him anywhere. I even tried calling him but he's not answering," she said. "It's like he's disappeared off the face of the earth."

I turned to Tyler. "We've got to track down Aunt Amber's photographer right away. The shooter must have been behind Aunt Amber when she was getting her pictures done. Maybe he or she will be in the background."

Tyler nodded. "With all the cameras everywhere, it's hard to believe we don't have any footage of Dirk's murder. And now with Steven's murder, things are spiraling out of control."

It was true. I expected Brayden to march through the door at any moment to fire Tyler. I turned to Aunt Amber. "Okay, I'll see if I can get you a lawyer. You'll need a good one to beat a double murder charge."

"What? No. You want my photographer?" Aunt Amber asked. "I can find him in a jiffy."

I walked over to her. "But you just said before you had no idea where he was."

"I suddenly remembered. I'm willing to do whatever it takes to get —I mean, help solve the case." She glared at Tyler as she extracted a business card from her pocket and handed it to Tyler.

"I'm going to try calling him." Tyler took the card and pointed at Aunt Amber. "Don't let her go anywhere, Cen. I'll be back in a minute."

We watched him leave and then shut the door behind him.

"He can't just hold me against my will can he?" Aunt Amber protested. "I am cooperating, Cen. Maybe you should call that lawyer after all."

"You're not actually locked up right now, in case you haven't noticed. And you brought all this on yourself. You never should have confessed in front of Brayden. You know he just wants a fast conviction, anything to make it all go away."

"I was just trying to lighten the mood. Look where it got me." Aunt Amber fluttered her eyelashes and wiped an imaginary tear from her cheek. "It was a false confession, coerced out of me under duress."

"You can't say stuff like that, Aunt Amber. It makes Tyler look bad. He's probably going to lose his job, and you're not helping make things better. The only way to fix everything is to solve the killings. Where is this photographer?"

Aunt Amber didn't answer and turned away. I moved closer, trying to see what she was doing. Her back faced me as she wiggled her shoulders and moved her arms back and forth. She spoke in a low voice in measured tones.

Find my photos and the taker,
Bring them here, safe and safer,
Please make haste and bring the maker,
Ready to deliver
From past, present, future.

I immediately recognized the Boomerang spell, though I had never attempted it myself. It was an intermediate spell that was well above my abilities. It also came with grave consequences if done improperly. Intermediate spells worked on people as well as things, so mistakes could be costly. The spell was both touchy and powerful, since it potentially changed both the present and the future.

I had no idea why Aunt Amber wanted to summon the photographer in addition to the photographs, but maybe that's what you did when you didn't know an object's exact location. If I had paid attention during my lessons, I would probably already know that.

We waited.

And waited.

Nothing happened.

"It's been so long that I've lost my touch." Aunt Amber sobbed into her hands. "I spent all that time on acting lessons at the expense of my magic. I've taken my craft for granted, all for a longshot movie career that's dead in the water. Oh, Cen, what have I done?"

I placed my arm around her shoulders. "It's okay, Aunt Amber. Maybe you're just having a bad day." I was very concerned, though. Aunt Amber never had trouble with her spells.

Her shoulders heaved as she sobbed uncontrollably. "I'm too upset. Nothing's working."

"Let me try." I figured that anything that went wrong could be fixed by Aunt Amber. I repeated the spell, not really expecting much.

Within seconds a mist rose from the floor around the two of us, enveloping us in a gray-green cloud. Seconds later it dissipated, and I locked eyes with a tall, slender, green-eyed man with receding blond hair. It was Aunt Amber's stills photographer from earlier in the day.

My heart stuck in my throat. Why had my spell worked and not Aunt Amber's? If I didn't know what I had done differently, how would I be able to undo it and send him back later? What if I couldn't put things back to normal?

"What the heck just happened?" The photographer scanned his surroundings. "How did I get here?"

"Relax," Aunt Amber said. "We just need to ask you a few questions. And get those pictures of yours."

"B-but they're still in my camera. I haven't done anything with them yet." He glared at Aunt Amber. "You drugged my coffee, didn't you?"

Aunt Amber shook her head. "No, but don't worry. Everything is fine. I'll explain later. Right now we need to see those pictures."

He looked down at his camera, surprised to see the strap hanging from his neck. "Wait a sec. I left my camera on my desk. How did it get here? Am I being kidnapped? What do you want?"

"The pictures, dummy. Just hand over the memory card and nobody gets hurt." Aunt Amber held out her hand as she tapped her foot impatiently.

The photographer fiddled with his camera and extracted the memory card, which he handed to Aunt Amber. "I still don't understand what's going on."

"Shhhh." She pressed a finger to his lips. "Give me a minute, okay?"

"Aunt Amber! You can't—"

The door flew open and Tyler marched in, his face red with anger. "Where did he come from? You can't use mag—" Tyler knew we were witches, but he didn't realize how much we could help him.

Or how much he needed us right now.

CHAPTER 25

Tyler rubbed his palms against his forehead. "This is getting worse and worse. You can't fix things with witchcraft. It just obscures the truth. I have no idea what's real and what's not anymore."

I patted his hand. "I promise I'll make sure things don't get out of hand." I worried they already had though. I had no control over anyone in my family, especially when it concerned witchcraft, but Tyler didn't need to know that.

"I think these are the photos you were looking for." Aunt Amber handed Tyler the memory card. "Better check them out first before I let this guy go."

The photographer studied Tyler's uniform. "Are you a real cop? Where am I?"

"Of course he's real," Aunt Amber snapped. "You're in Westwick Corners, silly. You took my photos, remember?"

"But I remember leaving this afternoon…" He frowned. "This isn't part of the movie, is it?"

Nobody answered.

"What the hell is happening to me?" The photographer broke out into a cold sweat. "Do I need a lawyer?"

"No. You're free to leave anytime." Tyler dismissed him with a wave.

The photographer started towards the door, but his feet were stuck in place. He bent down to remove his shoes, but they wouldn't budge either. "Something's wrong. Why can't I move?"

"Do what he says, Amber. Send him back." Tyler glared at her.

"But what if all the photos aren't there? Then I'll just have to call him back again."

"Do what Tyler says, Aunt Amber." I suddenly remembered it was me that had cast the spell. Aunt Amber probably couldn't send him back even if she wanted to. "Uh-oh. I guess I have to do it."

I tried and tried, but nothing happened.

Aunt Amber gave it a half-hearted shot too.

Nothing.

"When can I go?" The photographer's impatience had morphed into fear. He rubbed his wedding band as sweat glistened on his fore- head. He looked as if he was about to have a panic attack. We had to get him out of here and fast.

"Relax." Aunt Amber waved her hand and mumbled something under her breath.

The photographer's feet suddenly broke free. He lost his balance and fell to the ground. He glanced around nervously before scram- bling to his feet.

"We'll get you back home in a jiffy," Aunt Amber turned to Tyler for approval. "I'll have to drive him back to Shady Creek myself."

"We have to let her go," I said. "There's no other way to get him back there without involving other people." If other people saw him, it could potentially alter their present and future destinies too.

Attempting new spells to fix our dilemma was certainly beyond my capabilities, and at least for the moment, Aunt Amber's too. Thank goodness the photographer had only come from Shady Creek and not somewhere further afield.

"Okay, fine. Make it quick and don't let anyone see you leave." Tyler had already pulled up pictures from the memory card on his laptop. He scanned through each one, squinting at the screen. Since the photos were of Aunt Amber, the focus was on her face and not the background, but the set behind her was clearly visible.

Our efforts to get the photos had already paid off. I tapped the screen. "Look at that window across the street. I see somebody there. Can you enlarge it?"

Tyler and I watched Aunt Amber and her photographer leave before he connected the large monitor and projected the image onto the wall screen.

The image was grainy, but there was definitely someone watching from one of the windows on the opposite side of the street. Whoever it was had a perfect angle to shoot Dirk Diamond. From a distance, it was impossible to tell if it was a man or a woman.

One thing was certain, though. The mystery person wasn't part of the script. The vacant store had been closed for over a year, the windows boarded up with plywood prior to the movie shoot. The boards had been removed only for filming. No one should have been inside that building. It wasn't part of the script, and it was unoccupied and locked up.

It took a while to sort out what was happening in the script at the exact time each photograph was taken, but we slowly pieced together a timeline from the background activity happening on set in Aunt Amber's photographs. Tyler clicked through each picture in order until we reached the moment just before Dirk was shot.

But by then, no one was lurking in the building across the street. The mystery figure had vanished into thin air.

I was beginning to doubt we would find anything. There had been no broken glass or open doors or windows. Maybe the figure was just an apparition or figment of both our imaginations.

Then I saw it. I jumped from my seat and tapped on the big screen. "It's a man, and he's up on the roof now." That explained why he didn't show up in the footage, since the roof was out of frame.

Tyler jumped from his seat. "You know the saying, a picture's worth a thousand words? Well, this one just might be worth a million bucks."

There was just one problem. The man didn't have a gun in his hand. It was painfully obvious to me that we didn't have all the photographs. I just hoped against hope that the photographer had a second memory card.

We had to unlock the puzzle before Tyler's fate was sealed.

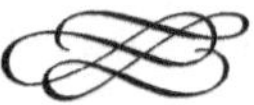

CHAPTER 26

Well over three hours had passed. It was after midnight and Aunt Amber still wasn't back. That worried me, since Aunt Amber drove like a NASCAR driver and Shady Creek was just an hour away. While she had been forced to physically drive the photographer back, she could have easily used witchcraft for her return trip.

Yet she still hadn't returned.

"Maybe she can get the photographer's second memory card without us having to bring him back." I was pretty sure my spell wouldn't work a second time. "I'll try to reach her."

Aunt Amber's cell phone went straight to voicemail. I willed her to call me but my telepathy skills were pathetic. I was feeling pretty down and out and even considered calling in Aunt Pearl and Mom for assistance.

Tyler tapped his watch. "It's going to be morning soon. I don't think Brayden's going to wait any longer, especially with all those people outside. I just wish we had more answers." He paced back and forth.

I sucked in my breath. "I'm going to try that spell one more time. Maybe I didn't ask for everything the first time."

"It's worth a shot," Tyler said. "What am I saying? I guess I'm so desperate, I'm agreeing with you."

"Okay, here I go." That made me want to try even harder. I took a deep breath and repeated the Boomerang spell. My skills were pretty hit or miss so I wasn't expecting the spell to work a second time. But at this point, we had everything to lose if something didn't happen quickly.

This time I visualized a stack of photographs and a pile of memory cards as I repeated the spell. If any occasion warranted using magic with reckless abandon, it was this one. I really didn't see how it could make matters any worse. It wasn't exactly cheating since the enhanced photographs would be made eventually. I was just speeding up the process.

I jumped as something popped behind me. The sound was a cross between popcorn and a crackling fire, except that it grew louder and faster until it finally exploded in a crescendo of sound.

A puff of gray-green smoke enveloped us. Tyler was barely visible across the table.

"Wow." Tyler coughed as the smoke dissipated. "That was spectacular."

"And effective too." I looked down at my hand, which contained another memory card and a dozen or so photographs. I wasn't sure if it was lucky or unlucky, but this time there was no freaked-out photographer or Aunt Amber.

The top photo showed Amber seated with the set in the background, similar to the ones we had seen on the last memory card. The next photo in the pile appeared to have been taken a few seconds after the first. They all appeared to be in sequence. The time frame of these new pictures paralleled the earlier ones, though these photos appeared to be ones that had been rejected due to poor exposure, composition, or other reasons. Maybe that was why they had been kept separate from the first batch. All of the photos in this latest batch had something wrong with them.

But one picture had everything right because a figure on the roof was clearly visible.

It was a man, his face obscured by a hoodie and scarf across his mouth and nose. No matter how much we enlarged the photograph, we couldn't make out his identity.

Tyler hunched over the table, squinting at the photograph. "I wish I recognized him, but I don't."

As I stood behind him, something jumped out at me. "Look at his hand. I've seen that ring before." It was a black signet ring. I couldn't make out the engraving, but it was very familiar to me. I just couldn't place where I had seen it before.

If only I could remember.

Tyler nodded. "Too bad we couldn't see more detail because that person has absolutely no reason to be there. All the actors are accounted for."

I squinted at the hand at the edge of the photograph, but it remained a mystery.

"We'll find the wearer, as long as they haven't taken off the ring," he said. "Maybe you can check everyone who's staying at the Inn, for starters."

That was the great thing about a small town like Westwick Corners. There were very few places to eat or drink. Sooner or later everybody ended up at the Inn's dining room or at the Witching Post's bar.

I checked my watch. It was three in the morning, but given today's events, maybe some late-night revelers were still around. "I'll head over there now."

"One more thing." Tyler slid a file folder across the table. "I have more bad news. Steven Scarabelli had a million-dollar policy on Dirk Diamond, just like Bill said. He also had one on Dirk's wife, Rose Lamont."

"That's not so uncommon, is it? After all, Rose and Dirk were

Steven Scarabelli's two biggest stars. If something happens to them, an insurance policy avoids financial disaster. A lot of businesses do that. That way no matter what, Steven could use the proceeds to pay the cast and crew."

"That won't happen anytime soon," Tyler said. "The money will go to Steven's estate first. I guess the actors will have to sue to get paid. There's something I think you should know, Cen."

"What?" I never suspected Tyler was holding anything back from me.

"We've got three people dead now if you count Rose Lamont's aneurysm."

I gasped. "You think Rose's death might be from something other than a brain aneurysm?"

"I don't know, Cen. But the timing's interesting. Two spouses die within a week of each other, and they have no kids. Rose in partic-ular—she was only in her thirties. Statistically, that is highly unusual."

"That's true," I said. "Rose and Dirk were mega-stars. I wonder who inherits their fortune."

"I wondered too." Tyler tapped the manila file folder. "I checked, and you'd never guess in a million years."

"Who?"

"Amber West. Looks like she was a good friend of Dirk's after all."

I felt like I was going to faint. "How is that possible? Dirk and his wife leave their fortune to her, yet Dirk wants her fired from the movie?"

Tyler shrugged. "Maybe she's a good friend but a bad actor?"

"She never mentioned any inheritance." Maybe she hadn't exagger-ated their friendship after all. But until the movie, she had never even mentioned Dirk Diamond by name. Yet apparently they were so close that she was named as his life insurance beneficiary. It was almost like she had a secret life that no one in our family knew about. "Maybe she didn't know about it."

"Or it could explain why she's so late coming back. Maybe she decided not to return after all." Tyler stood and paced back and forth. "She knows she'll have to answer a lot of questions."

"No, that's not possible. How can you even say that?" I frowned. "She would never leave her family. Besides, she has to actually collect the money, right?"

"True, but you can do that through lawyers and stuff," Tyler said. "I'm not accusing her, just stating the obvious. If it's true, anyone can see she stood to gain from Dirk's death. What is their relationship, exactly? How long did she know Dirk?"

I threw my hands up in defeat. "No idea. I only found out today that she knew any of them. She never talked about them before, but apparently they've all been friends forever. I've always known that she likes to be the center of attention but had no clue she did any kind of acting. Or that she gave Dirk his 'lucky' break." I made quote marks in the air.

I guess I didn't really know my aunt at all.

"Maybe Amber's not so lucky," Tyler said. "She still has to live long enough to collect it."

CHAPTER 27

I finally left Tyler in the interview room after waiting a while longer for Aunt Amber's return. But when hours passed and she still hadn't come back, I grew increasingly worried. If she really was an heir to the Diamond fortune, she now had a price on her head.

I stepped out into the dark lobby and immediately collided with an invisible force. A man's chest, to be exact. My pulse quickened as arms clamped onto my biceps.

"Let go of me!" I screamed as I tried to spin around but it was no use. I couldn't break free.

"Relax! Why are you freaking out like that? I'm just trying to keep you from falling." He loosened his grip and took a step back. I smelled alcohol on his breath.

I recognized the voice—and drunken slur—of Rick Mazure. "How did you get in here?" Maybe Aunt Amber had left the door unlocked in her rushed departure.

"I convinced the security guard to let me in. I urgently need to talk to Sheriff Gates. Is he here? There's something I have to tell him."

I exhaled, feeling like an idiot. "You thought of something else since you met with him earlier? Is it something new?"

"Not exactly." Rick looked down at his shoes, uneasy. "I'm a bit conflicted about the whole thing. I like Steven Scarabelli, but…"

The door clicked open. Tyler stood in the doorway. "What did you say about Scarabelli?"

Rick frowned. "It's confidential. Shouldn't we go inside your office?"

"Actually, I was just leaving," Tyler turned the key in the door and locked it. "You can walk with me."

"B-but I don't think—" Rick cast an uneasy glance at me.

"Whatever you have to say can be said in front of Cendrine. She's helping me with the investigation."

Rick looked alarmed as he studied me. "Is that normal? I mean, you're not a detective or anything."

"It's all hands on deck," Tyler said. "I deputized her."

He had done no such thing, but I knew Tyler wanted me as a witness to Rick's statements. Not only that but if Tyler waited till morning, Rick might change his mind about talking.

Rick scanned the lobby to make sure no one else was around. "It's no secret that Dirk gave Scarabelli a bum deal. Dirk's constant demands infuriated everyone. Scarabelli was very patient with him, but I guess he finally reached the point where he just couldn't take it anymore."

"Did Steven confide in you?" I felt a sickening feeling in my stomach. More evidence that pointed towards Steven Scarabelli. By now Brayden knew that Tyler had released Steven Scarabelli. Steven's dead body at the Inn was proof of that. Releasing a killer could be the nail in the coffin, so to speak. Even with Steven dead, Brayden would accuse Tyler of incompetence, or worse. I shuddered.

"Steven didn't come right out and say it, exactly. I mean, not literally." Rick bit his lip. "But he did say yesterday that he'd had enough, and that he'd make sure that Dirk never made another movie as long as he lived."

"There's lots of ways to interpret that other than a death threat," Tyler said. "Maybe Steven didn't want to work with him anymore. It sounds like nobody else in Hollywood wanted to work with him either."

Rick laughed. "People will put up with anything for enough money. Even Dirk Diamond doesn't seem so bad when there's millions to be made."

"You're saying Steven Scarabelli killed Dirk Diamond?" Steven hardly struck me as a killer. Pretty much every member of the cast and crew had remarked on how kind and honest Steven was, and that he would do anything to help another person. He had even helped Dirk, despite the abuse he got in return.

Rick shrugged. "You really can't blame the guy. Dirk had it coming."

Tyler frowned. "Do you have proof to back up your suspicions?"

"I overheard Steven and Amber arguing. Amber claimed she would inherit Dirk's fortune and she refused to share anything with Steven. I was kind of shocked to discover that Amber was a beneficiary in Dirk's will. After thinking it over, I realized it was important enough to mention," Rick said. "I'm just sorry I didn't say anything sooner."

I flashed back to their earlier argument. Rick's claim tied in with Tyler's comment. Was there more to the conversation than just Aunt Amber's firing?

"What exactly did you hear?" Tyler penciled some notes on his notepad.

Rick glanced furtively around the empty lobby. "Can't we just—"

Tyler shook his head. "The sooner you tell me, the better."

Rick sighed. "Okay, look, Steven got backed into a corner and he was desperate. He was in trouble with the investors that were backing the movie. When Dirk quit and Steven still had to pay the cast and crew, he was screwed. The investors were out their money and they weren't too happy about it. Steven had to find money, and fast."

I suddenly remembered the ring. I glanced at Rick's hands, but his fingers on both hands were bare.

"I hesitated to come forward because Steven is my friend," Rick said. "But then Steven said he was going to kill Dirk. I didn't take him seriously at first, but then he started asking all sorts of questions about the weapons in the script and stuff. That struck me as strange at the time, but it wasn't until now that I put all the pieces together."

"You think Steven planted a loaded gun?" Tyler's eyes narrowed.

"In light of what happened, it sure seems that way. I know Steven was desperate, but I thought he was all talk. That he would just decide to stop making films with Dirk or something. Until, well...I never thought he'd actually kill someone. I guess Dirk finally drove him to do it."

It dawned on me that Steven couldn't exactly confirm or deny Rick's claims now that he was dead. But all the pieces seemed to fit together.

Except for the shadowy figure on the roof, who was decidedly smaller and slimmer than Steven Scarabelli.

"You're making a bold assumption," Tyler said. "But we'll look into it."

"It's no assumption, Sheriff Gates." Rick kicked at a chip in the marble floor. "Steven just carried through on his threat."

"Why didn't you say anything earlier?" Tyler asked.

"I don't know...maybe somehow I thought Dirk deserved it. I mean, he was a really mean guy, and if anyone had it coming, it was him. He messed things up horribly for Steven. But no one deserves to die."

"No, they don't," I said softly. "No matter how badly they treat other people." No one deserves to be a scapegoat either, especially when they were so conveniently dead.

Life was unfair sometimes. Apparently so was death.

CHAPTER 28

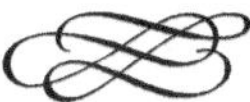

The once bustling streets outside City Hall were now dark and deserted, a sharp contrast from earlier. Tyler had returned to his office to validate Rick's information. I walked alone, my heels clicking on the empty sidewalk as I thought about Rick's claims. I had forgotten to ask him if anyone else was close enough to overhear Steven and Amber's argument.

It seemed like forever to reach my car though it was only two blocks away. I had parked on the adjacent street just so it wouldn't be obvious to Brayden that I was at the police station with Tyler. I didn't expect him to return to the office at this late hour, but I couldn't be sure. The last thing I wanted was to antagonize him further. That just made things worse for Tyler.

I increased my pace when I spotted my rusty and trusty old Honda waiting under the lone functioning streetlight on the block, looking sad and lonely.

I dropped my purse onto the passenger seat, jumped in the driver's seat, and turned the ignition. I pulled out of the parking spot and floored the gas pedal, knowing I wouldn't get stopped for a speeding ticket. I sped through town and was relieved to see that the Dirk fans had abandoned their post for the night too. I turned up the driveway and headed up the hill to the Inn.

It was probably too late, but I wanted to check everyone's hands while they were still in the dining room or at The Witching Post. Some people might have already left town, thinking that the movie couldn't continue. Others would have retired to their rooms for the night. But I could probably still catch a few of them.

I parked my car and ran across the driveway to The Witching Post. The music and voices that drifted outside told me that we still had a full house.

I spotted Arianne first. She sat at the bar with Rick Mazure, who had beaten me to the bar by only a few minutes. My pace quickened as I walked towards them. I stopped suddenly. Something told me to back off.

I nodded at Rick and Arianne and slid into an empty seat a few feet away on Rick's left. I smiled at Aunt Pearl, who was bartending. She nodded at me, then turned her back. A split second later, she wordlessly dropped a coaster on the bar in front of me followed by a glass of red wine. She was uncharacteristically quiet as she retreated to the opposite end of the bar to serve beers to a couple of locals.

Even over the loud country music, I could tell Rick Mazure was already drunker than a skunk again. He had seemed to sober up somewhat at City Hall, but in just fifteen minutes he was back to his former state. Maybe it was understandable given that he was suddenly out of a job. Or maybe Aunt Pearl was up to her old tricks again. I strained my ears to hear their conversation.

"What was I saying?" Rick's words slurred as he tossed back his glass and drained the rest of his whisky.

"You were telling me how you were going to make me a star." Arianne Duval twirled her plastic cocktail stir stick. She sounded a little sarcastic, like she wasn't buying whatever it was that Rick was selling.

"A star? You'll be the whole damn constellation." He placed his hand on top of Arianne's. "I got a great series idea, but it's a secret right now."

I wondered if it was the same script that Rick had been pitching to Dirk earlier.

Arianne Duval lifted her hand at the pretense of stirring her drink. "What's the premise?"

I studied her hands. While she had rings on both hands, they were far more delicate than the one in the photograph. And her rings were gold, not silver.

Rick leaned towards her. "Girl down on her luck, discovered in a drugstore. You're just perfect for the role."

"Let me guess. A Hollywood and Vine setting?" Arianne didn't wait for a reply. "You're kidding me, right? It's all been done before."

"Everything's been done before, Arianne. It's a formula, and I know how to work it. That's the reason Dirk got so successful. My writing is what made him shine. I'll make you famous too."

"I'm famous already. You've got to do better than that."

"Hitch your wagon to me and I'll guarantee you'll be putting your feet in cement, and fans will be stepping in your footsteps on the Hollywood Walk of Fame."

Arianne rolled her eyes. "I think you're giving yourself a little too much credit."

"Look, I know how to write a blockbuster. In fact, it's already written." Rick tapped his glass for a refill. "It's not like you have anything else going on. You want in on it or not?

Arianne was silent for a moment as she sipped her drink. "Maybe."

"I wouldn't wait too long if I were you. Kim's finding me more talent right now, as we speak," he said.

"Okay, fine. I'll take a look at the script." Arianne downed the rest of her drink. "What have I got to lose?"

"You're in." Rick held out his hand. "Let's shake on it."

Arianne shook his hand as Rick pulled a sheaf of papers from his jacket and stuck them in front of her. "This script is for your eyes only. Promise you won't breathe a word of it."

Arianne nodded.

"Good," he said. "I'll have a contract drawn up for you in the morning. I can pretty much print money with my scripts. Everybody's going to be sorry they didn't take me more seriously."

I had a feeling some people already were.

CHAPTER 29

Aunt Pearl caught my attention with a wave, motioning me over to the opposite end of the bar. I got up from my seat and headed towards her with my wineglass. I sat down on a stool next to Kim Antonelli. She glared at me and I dropped my gaze to her hands, one of which cradled a drink.

No rings.

Kim slammed her margarita glass down on the bar, spilling green liquid all over the bar. "It's not fair. Dirk Diamond was my only client. He monopolized all my time until I gave up all my business. Now he's gone and all of a sudden I've dropped to zero income. I'm basically out of a job."

Her rant seemed more for show than anything. The words and actions were there, but there seemed to be no emotion behind it.

"Maybe you should have diversified." Aunt Pearl placed a coaster on the bar in front of me, followed by a frosty glass of cold water. "Having only one client is a recipe for disaster."

"Maybe you should mind your own business," she snapped. Her anger towards Aunt Pearl at least seemed genuine.

I frowned at Aunt Pearl before turning to Kim. "Who do you think killed Dirk?"

Kim threw her hands in the air. "Who knows? Everybody—and I mean everybody—hated him. Even his wife Rose. She wanted a divorce, but he promised to make her live to regret it. Only she died, because he killed her."

I gasped. "You think Dirk killed Rose?"

"I know he did," Kim said. "He didn't want to lose any money in a divorce. He even said as much. He said the only way his marriage would end was if one of them died."

I motioned to Aunt Pearl to bring Kim a refill. I had to keep her talking. "I guess he got what he wanted. For a while, at least."

I remembered Tyler's comments about Aunt Amber being the sole heir. "Did Dirk have a will?"

Kim nodded but didn't elaborate.

I gulped my water, the cold liquid soothing my parched throat. "Who inherits?"

Kim glanced around and lowered her voice. "I do."

I choked on my water, spewing it all over the bar and adding to the green liquid puddle in front of us. Kim's claim conflicted with Tyler's. "You inherit everything?"

Kim frowned. "That's what Dirk's lawyer told me when I called him about Dirk's death. Apparently, Rose's estate went to Dirk, but then when Dirk died, I was bequeathed everything after Rose."

I was a little surprised that Kim would have called his lawyer already. And that the lawyer would have told her. But maybe Hollywood agents managed a lot of personal stuff for big-name stars like Dirk.

Aunt Pearl arrived with a towel and mopped up the mess. She took Kim's glass and replaced it with a fresh margarita.

Kim promptly downed half her drink.

Or maybe Kim and Dirk's relationship was more than professional. "You must have been surprised about his will." It struck me as odd that she had apparently just inherited millions, yet still worried about losing her job.

"A little. I thought maybe he did it as a temporary thing when Rose filed for divorce, but the lawyer said no, Dirk had changed everything without consulting him. That was typical Dirk, but it still blows my mind that he would leave me his fortune. I know what you're thinking, but Dirk and I were strictly professional. Ask anyone. Who knows why he left everything to me? Dirk did weird things like that sometimes. I just worked for him."

"Rose filed for divorce?" If that was true, then maybe Rose's death wasn't accidental. Dirk had a strong motive to kill her. Yet both her death and divorce proceedings hadn't been reported in the media. My head was spinning with all the conflicting information. Somebody, or maybe even everybody, was lying. Both Rick and Tyler believed that Amber was Dirk's heir. Yet Kim claimed otherwise. How many times had Dirk changed his will?

Dirk had probably counted on Kim's loyalty for some reason. Or just knew that he could control her. No decent lawyer would advise a client to make such an arrangement, so naturally he had wanted to keep the change to his will secret—never expecting he would actually die while his temporary arrangement was in place.

"Who knew Dirk had changed his will?" I asked.

Kim threw her hands in the air. "No idea. I certainly didn't know. Maybe no one did except Dirk. He was very secretive about certain things."

We both jumped as something crashed behind the bar, followed by breaking glass. A shelf had collapsed, sending bottles of expensive liqueurs smashing to the floor.

"Oops!" Aunt Pearl surveyed the damage, sounding suspiciously cheery. "I can fix that in a jiffy."

I held up my hand, fearing she was up to no good. "You're not going to—"

But Aunt Pearl was already whispering a rewind spell. "One, two, three…make it not to be…"

Kim appeared not to notice. Not that it really mattered. A rewind spell only erased Kim's recent memory and reset everything back to moments earlier. History would just repeat itself as the erased moments were relived.

I was annoyed with Aunt Pearl because I had been making real progress with Kim. I hated to start questioning her all over again. It just wasted valuable time when we couldn't afford any delays. But start all over I did until I reached the same point in our conversation.

"Kim, were you and Dirk having an affair?" I watched her carefully, looking for any slips in her expression or body language.

"What? No! He's so old! I know he's a star and all, but he's twice my age! Besides, I would never steal another woman's husband." Kim's slurred words grew louder. The rewind spell had somehow reversed history without restoring her sobriety.

"But he left you all his money…."

"Oh, that." She waved her hand in dismissal. "I'm sure it won't really come to me. He just did that until he could figure out what to do next. After Rose died, he decided to leave his money to charity but he didn't know which one. So he put my name in there just for a month or so while he figured it out. It'll be contested, I'm sure."

Even more of a bombshell the second time around. Her answer had changed oh so slightly before and after Aunt Pearl's rewind spell. Which meant she was lying the first time.

"And if anything happened while he was figuring things out…you stood to inherit millions." If Kim really was behind Dirk's death, she had a very short window of time to execute her plan. "As it turns out, you did."

"Are you accusing me of killing Dirk? I don't believe this." Kim traced her finger around the rim of her margarita glass and licked the salt from her finger. She smacked her lips. "I'm the last person who would have done such a thing. I'm the only person he trusted in the end."

"So you were friends?"

"Well, the closest thing to a friend, since Dirk didn't have any. I'm the only one he confided in. I knew things about him that even his wife didn't."

"Like what?" Whatever she was to him, she didn't seem sorry he was gone. I supposed that the promise of all his money eased the pain a little.

Kim paused for a few seconds, considering what to say. "Dirk planned to start his own production company and make his own movies, rather than working for Steven. That's the real reason he was so difficult and why he wanted to quit. He delayed things as much as possible because he didn't want Steven's movie to compete with the movie his new company was about to make."

"Let me guess...a new action thriller?" I flashed back to Rick Mazure's suspicions about Steven Scarabelli. Maybe there was something to it.

"Yep." Kim leaned back on her barstool, almost losing her balance before grabbing the bar to steady herself. Whatever feelings everyone had for Dirk, his passing had triggered a universal desire to get drunk.

"Does anyone else know about Dirk's new company?" Again things pointed to Steven. If in fact, he already knew of Dirk's betrayal.

Kim shrugged. "I doubt it. Dirk wanted it kept secret until he was ready to pull the plug."

"Too bad he didn't live long enough to do that," I said. "That might have spared him."

"I don't see how that has anything to do with their deaths." Kim looked as if she was personally offended. As the person who stood to inherit Dirk's millions, she wouldn't say anything to incriminate herself.

"What if somebody did know?" I doubted it was a coincidence. "Dirk walks, and a bunch of people are out of a job. Dirk had lots of enemies. Maybe even some who wanted to kill him. Can you think of anyone who would actually carry it out?"

"I didn't want to say it, but there is one." Kim lowered her voice. "Amber West had threatened him about acting roles. She seemed to think he owed her favors or something. Always having a temper tantrum if she didn't get what she wanted. That woman is a piece of work."

"Hmm." I hid my shock as best I could. I just wanted to keep Kim talking, but it pained me to hear her deflect blame onto other people, my aunt in particular. Judging by her comments, she had no idea that Amber was my aunt, or that Aunt Pearl and Aunt Amber were sisters.

Aunt Pearl inched closer and wiped the bar with a cloth. "Amber's just passionate about her craft. She's such a talented actress."

I frowned at Aunt Pearl. Her exaggerated comments were sure to trigger Kim.

Kim acknowledged her with a nod and then turned back to me. "The more I think about it, the more I'm sure Amber did it. That woman has a crazy temper. She looks like a sweet little old lady, but she's really mean."

Everyone seemed to point fingers at Aunt Amber, yet that couldn't be. She had no time to kill Dirk, and she had seemed genuinely surprised when we discovered Steven dead in his room. It couldn't be true, but it worried me all the same. Amber had admitted being upstairs around the time when Steven was killed.

I couldn't recall if Kim had been in the dining room at the time of Aunt Amber's false confession, but she could have been. Or maybe she had heard about it from someone else.

"Let me get this straight. You think Dirk killed Rose, and Amber killed Dirk? What's the motive?" Especially since Kim ended up with Dirk's money, I wanted to add.

"Who knows? Amber's old and crazy." Kim twirled her index finger by her ear. "She'll do anything to get what she wants."

"Amber's not old!" Aunt Pearl's face reddened. Aunt Pearl was the oldest of the three sisters, a few years older than Aunt Amber. If Amber was old, that made her even older.

Kim frowned. "Sure she is…she must be at least sixty. I guess some people don't mellow with old age. Did you know that she threw a chair at Steven? She was so mean to him, yet he still kept her on as an extra. That's the kind of person Steven was. Loyal to a fault."

An extra?

I suddenly realized that Kim had completely changed the subject to focus on Aunt Amber instead of her. It also dawned on me that if Dirk made his own movies, he no longer needed an agent to find him acting roles. Maybe Kim was more involved than she let on.

And, despite her claims about Aunt Amber, she had provided important new information that, if verified, could clear Aunt Amber for good. But I feared a free Aunt Amber might just do more harm than good.

CHAPTER 30

Kim stood and grabbed her purse off the bar. "I've had it with this hick town. See you around sometime." She pulled out her wallet and peeled off a few bills, which she dropped on the bar.

Aunt Pearl, who had been cleaning up the broken glass nearby, called after her. "Wait—you forgot something!"

"No, I've got everything." Kim frowned.

Aunt Pearl held up a necklace. "You must have dropped this."

Kim retraced her steps and grabbed the silver chain. She studied it momentarily before opening the clasp and sliding off the pendant.

My mouth dropped open as I recognized the pendant. It really wasn't a pendant at all, just a silver signet ring that hung on the chain. "Where did you get that?"

Kim tilted her head towards the opposite end of the bar. "Ask that guy." She removed the ring and rolled it on its side down the bar.

Rick Mazure jumped from his seat and ran to the middle of the bar, where the ring stood on end for a split second before jangling to a stop. He clamped his hand over the ring and picked it up.

"Is that yours?" I walked slowly towards him while I texted Tyler on my cell phone. I had just started to type when the bar door opened.

Tyler walked in, unnoticed by Rick or the other bar patrons.

Rick shoved the ring in his pocket. "Of course it's mine."

"It looks a lot like my boyfriend's ring. Let me see it." Rick didn't know that Tyler was my boyfriend. I needed to stall long enough for Tyler to arrive, so I made up a long story about how I had bought the ring for my boyfriend and he was always misplacing it.

Rick pulled the ring from his pocket. "It's mine all right. See the initial R? That's proof."

Tyler had walked up quietly behind us.

"That's proof all right," I said. "You killed Dirk Diamond and that ring proves it. We've got everything on film."

"What? You're crazy." Rick scowled. "What is it with this crazy town? I told Dirk we should never have come here. It was all Steven's idea, influenced by that crazy Amber."

"I think you told Dirk exactly the opposite," I said. "What better place to kill him than a one-horse town with a limited police presence."

Aunt Pearl reached up and turned off the music. Not that she had to, because by now everyone in the bar had overheard our conversation. Most of them were already out of their seats, walking towards us in disbelief.

I glanced at Tyler.

He nodded as he moved between Rick and the door. "Rick Mazure, you're under arrest for the murders of Dirk Diamond and Steven Scarabelli." He read a stunned Rick his Miranda rights.

"You're not really going to listen to her, are you?" Rick swore under his breath.

I smiled at him. "Everyone was frustrated with Dirk's ridiculous demands and the way he treated people," I said. "But no one more than you. Dirk treated you the worst of all. You worked like a dog with his constant rewrites, yet he never so much as thanked you."

He shrugged. "He was a jerk, so what? We all knew that going in, and Steven paid us well. Why would I kill the golden goose?"

"You were frustrated with all the rushed changes," Tyler said. "Who could blame you? While everyone else sat around waiting for Dirk's latest demands to be written into the script, you were writing away furiously. He worked you almost to death, didn't he?"

Rick shrugged. "That's my job. After all, Dirk was the star of the show. Have to keep the stars happy."

"But everyone has a limit, Rick. Yours came when you and Dirk worked on a project together. He started his own production company and hired you to write his first script. You worked day and night to write it on top of your day job, yet Dirk ended up rejecting it."

Rick flushed but didn't respond.

"That was the final straw, wasn't it?" Tyler asked. "Dirk was ungrateful. He tricked you, but you got the ultimate revenge on Dirk by writing his murder into the scene."

"No, you've got it all wrong. I started my own company and was planning to leave—"

Tyler shook his head. "You got that idea only after you killed Dirk. But things got complicated when Steven became suspicious about the weapons in the heist changing from knives into guns. That's when he started to wonder what was going on."

Rick held up a hand in protest. "Steven was too busy to care. He asked me to work directly with Dirk."

Tyler continued. "There was another problem with the guns. Steven knew the guns were all blanks. Bill had his faults, but Steven had worked with him long enough to know that Bill would never have a loaded gun on set."

Bill nodded from where he stood a few feet away. Everyone had left their seats and formed a loose semi-circle around us.

Rick shook his head. "Steven's supposed to approve all the rewrites. He knew about the changes."

"No, that's not what happened," I said. "You knew he wouldn't read it ahead of time because he had trusted you before. Steven was too busy getting everyone's contracts signed and didn't have time to look at each script change. I heard him tell you to just go ahead."

Tyler nodded. "Despite Steven not signing off on your rewrites, it was obvious that changing the weapons from knives to guns was pretty major. Steven knew that wasn't something Dirk had requested. Dirk's changes were always about making Dirk look good, not something as basic as the weapons used."

"No! You have it all wrong," Rick protested. "Dirk asked for the craziest things, and I had to write them in."

"Steven confronted you, didn't he?" Tyler didn't wait for an answer. "Once he knew what you had done, he was about to expose you. You had no choice but to kill him too. That way no one else would find out you killed Dirk. You went to Steven's room and found him alone."

Rick bent over and buried his face in his hands. He sobbed uncontrollably. "Steven was my friend."

"But the real thing that gave you away is your signet ring," I said. "You wore it when you shot Dirk. You got rid of it because you were afraid it was tainted with gunpowder residue. So you gave it to Kim."

Rick's mouth dropped open. He could hardly deny it was his after claiming it at the bar.

Kim paled as her hand flew to her chest. "No!"

"Then you tried to frame a dead man by blaming Steven for Dirk's death, and accusing Amber of killing Steven. Too bad your plan wasn't as tight as your movie plots." I flashed back to the morning when I had been carrying Aunt Amber's dresses. That's when I had first seen Rick's ring, though I had forgotten all about it until now.

"It all makes sense now," Bill said. "My missing gun, and the ridiculous changes like the horse and the guns. I had no choice but to leave my props unattended. Otherwise it would hold up the movie shoot. That gave Rick ample opportunity to steal a gun and load it with live ammunition."

"By the time Dirk realized the changes were screw-ups, he would already be dead." Arianne wiped a tear from her cheek. "And we were all so anxious to get this scene shot that we were all scrambling. I guess that's why I had to get my own gun from the prop box." She nodded sympathetically at Bill.

"Rick rewrote the scene to add other guns as a distraction." Tyler pulled handcuffs from his jacket pocket and placed them on Rick's wrists. He turned Rick around and pointed at him. "You figured the gunfire chase scene would cover up the real bullet you fired, but you made one major mistake. You didn't take into account the bullet's trajectory. Based on where it hit Dirk, it came not from the set, but from across the street."

"I guess you thought no one would notice," I said. "But Bill certainly noticed his missing gun. You couldn't replace it in the gun case without being discovered. You only had time to drop it in the big prop box."

"Why'd you do it, Rick?" Bill shook his head. "We all had a good thing going."

Rick lunged unsteadily at Bill, unable to balance while handcuffed. Tyler stepped in between them.

"Why? Because I don't steal and I think thieves should have to pay. Dirk stole my idea for a new series I wrote especially for him. He promised me he'd make me rich, but when I wrote the scripts he just stole them from me and cut me out of the deal. He just made a multi-million dollar television deal on the series I wrote, but he stiffed me on the payment." Rick's face flushed with anger. "My scripts made him a star in the first place, and that's what I get?"

"I'm sure he would have paid you eventually." I doubted it myself but wanted to inject some calm into the situation.

Rick shook his head. "No. He not only left my name off the credits but claimed he wrote it himself! He was nothing but a thief, a common criminal."

"But he was such a huge star," Aunt Pearl said. "He didn't need your stupid script."

Rick's face reddened. "My stupid scripts are what got him famous in the first place. Without me, he was nothing."

CHAPTER 31

I followed behind Tyler in my Honda as he drove a handcuffed Rick to the jail.

Only the cell was already occupied—by an uncharacteristically conscientious Aunt Amber. She had returned while we were at the Witching Post. And apparently locked herself back in the cell for some reason. She gripped the bars with both hands as she swore under her breath. "I can't believe I missed all the action."

Tyler handed me the keys and I unlocked the door. I grabbed Aunt Amber's hand and escorted her from the cell so that Tyler could place Rick inside. "You're coming with me."

I guided her through the door and out into the outer office.

"What happens now?" Aunt Amber dabbed a tear from her eye. "Everything I've worked for is gone. The movie is never going to get made."

"You were a last-minute addition," I pointed out. "You don't have that much invested in the movie. I mean, you used witchcraft to memorize your lines."

She shrugged. "Just because I'm naturally talented doesn't mean it was easy. I flew all the way from London. And I had to skip Ruby's desserts all this week to keep my figure. All that suffering for nothing."

I could argue that she hadn't suffered at all, but that would get me nowhere. Instead, I patted her arm. "I'm sorry, Aunt Amber. What can I do to cheer you up?"

She batted her eyelashes, her sobbing stopped. "I know the movie is not 'in the can', but can't we have a wrap party?" She made air quotes with her fingers. "It's not our fault that we couldn't finish filming."

"I don't know. That seems a bit insensitive considering that Dirk, Rose, and Steven all met untimely deaths." The Los Angeles coroner had confirmed that Rose's death really was from a brain aneurysm. Dirk hadn't killed her. No one had. It was just a horrible, tragic coincidence that the husband and wife had worked on the same film and also died within days of each other. Their marital woes had first seemed to be a motive, but each of their deaths had been the result of other factors.

At least one of the mysterious deaths had a natural explanation. Hardly good news, just less bad news.

"I guess." She looked crestfallen. "What if we change the name of the movie? Add some new scenes?"

"Not a good idea," I said. "You just beat a murder charge. Maybe you should put your acting career on hold and lie low for now."

Aunt Amber brightened. "We'll have a red carpet memorial right here in town. All the Hollywood bigwigs will be invited to Westwick Corners. It will be the event of the season."

"Is that what Dirk or Steven would have wanted?" I frowned, thinking Aunt Pearl would likely set Main Street ablaze if any more visitors came to town.

Aunt Amber shrugged. "Who can say? They aren't here to tell us."

"You're right, they aren't. Let's leave it to their families to decide," I said.

"This just feels so…unfinished." Aunt Amber sighed. "My chance for an Oscar is gone forever."

"You'll always be a star in my eyes." Maybe I was exaggerating a little, but I just never understood why Aunt Amber sidelined her supernatural talents for an acting career. She was already a star in the witchcraft world.

I supposed that even a witch like Aunt Amber could want things she couldn't have, all the while overlooking the fact that she already had it all. "Fame isn't all it's cracked up to be."

"You're right, Cen. All the paparazzi, the fans…it's better to be ordinary." She sighed. "I'll just go back to my ordinary existence. At least I'm a free woman."

"And you helped me get an exclusive story. I was the last journalist to speak with Steven Scarabelli. In fact, I've already had calls from some of the Hollywood media." It was a lie meant to poke some fun at her, but I instantly regretted my words.

Aunt Amber primped her hair. "Really? Tell them to call me. I've got some juicy Hollywood gossip to share."

The office door opened and Mom and Aunt Pearl stepped inside.

"I heard the news." Mom hugged Aunt Amber. "I'm sorry your movie role didn't work out."

"Yeah, sorry." The only thing Aunt Pearl seemed apologetic about was having to say sorry in the first place.

"That's okay. They weren't paying me enough anyway. With everything that's happened I think I can hold out for a better deal." Aunt Amber was clearly basking in her newfound celebrity status.

Tyler emerged into the outer office and I stepped towards him. I whispered in his ear, "Make a big deal about her release, okay?"

Aunt Amber was already out in the lobby.

"Don't worry, Cen. Half of the Hollywood press is out in front of the building. They showed up a few minutes ago after I called Brayden about Rick Mazure's arrest." Tyler locked the door behind us as we headed out into the lobby.

I smiled. "I guess good news travels fast."

Tyler laughed. "I never knew that adulation was so important to

Amber. She didn't have to send us on false leads just to get attention. I mean, she can conjure up a crowd anytime she wants."

"True," I said. "But Aunt Amber has no idea the crowd is here for Rick Mazure's arrest—not her release. That's why this crowd is so special to her. It's real—not one she made up. As far as she's concerned, there's nothing quite like getting acquitted of murder to draw a crowd."

CHAPTER 32

The late morning sun warmed our shoulders as Mom and I stood by the city hall steps. We craned our necks to see past the crowd of media people who waited for Aunt Amber. She had suddenly achieved the stardom she had coveted, albeit in a way she had probably never imagined.

Yesterday's events already felt like a memory, though at least part of it was about to be replayed.

Aunt Amber had insisted on a reenactment of her late-night release together with a press conference and, surprisingly, Brayden had agreed. It seemed that my aunt's theatrics added flair to what would have been an otherwise boring press conference. And, no surprise—Brayden would take credit for Rick Mazure's capture and the freeing of my now proven innocent aunt.

I scanned the City Hall steps but saw no sign of Aunt Amber or Tyler for that matter. He found Brayden's antics humorous now that his job was safe once again. Tyler had dodged the bullet, so to speak. I just hoped that our luck held so that there were no more surprises from my ex-fiancé.

No one had yet emerged from the building for Mayor Brayden Banks' hastily arranged press conference. There were news vans from the major networks and reporters standing by in front of cameras with lighting. There were almost as many lights and cameras as there had been during the movie shoot.

Despite the sunlight, powerful camera lights erased every lingering morning shadow and lit up the city hall entrance brighter than Times Square on New Year's Eve. It kind of felt like we were all part of a low-budget reality show, waiting for a grand entrance or an outrageous plot twist.

I squinted and focused on the City Hall doors through the bright lights, camera equipment, and the gaggle of film crews and reporters that blocked our view. The media weren't just local journalists. Aside from a local Shady Creek reporter, I recognized the host of a popular Hollywood television entertainment show. He was getting his makeup retouched and looked strangely out of place in a suit and tie.

I glanced down at my wrinkled clothes, suddenly feeling grubby and tired. The last twenty-four hours had been crazy, to say the least. But things had finally come to a conclusion and I was grateful for that. Amber's charges were dropped, Rick Mazure was in jail, and Tyler got to keep his job. At least I hoped he did.

Whatever Mayor Brayden Banks did, at least he got a taste of humble pie.

"She's coming," someone whispered. People murmured, rustled and jostled as everyone got into position. The City Hall doors were about to open.

Mom linked her arm with mine. "Looks like Amber has finally gotten her fifteen minutes of fame. I just wish it hadn't come at such a high cost."

I nodded. "Nothing like being acquitted of murder to get your name in the news. I guess any publicity is good publicity."

"I just wish she hadn't wanted to be a movie star," Mom said. "Nobody would have come to Westwick Corners to make a movie.

Maybe none of this would have happened, and Dirk and Steven would still be alive."

"Not so."

I jumped at the voice behind me.

"That wouldn't have made much difference." Grandma Vi floated in front of us. "Rick would have worked with Dirk in another time or place. And he would have killed him. You must know that you can't change fate. All that changes is the details but never the outcome."

Aunt Pearl nodded. "Karma's a bitch sometimes."

Suddenly the large City Hall doors opened and I saw a flash of red hair as Aunt Amber came into view. She looked so tiny against the large doors. She was flanked by Mayor Brayden Banks on one side and Sheriff Tyler Gates on the other. They stood outside the doors at the top of the steps and faced the crowd.

Aunt Amber wore a long white evening gown with 1950s-era elbow length gloves. She gave the crowd a royal wave and slowly turned from left to right. "Thank you all for supporting me. I am free at last."

I must have snorted a little too loud because the people in front of us turned around.

"Cut the drama, already," Aunt Pearl said. "I've had enough excitement for one day."

"Shameless!" Grandma Vi cried. "She always did have to be the center of attention. Making up for being a middle child I guess."

Aunt Amber milked her time in the spotlight for all it was worth, taking questions from reporters and posing for the cameras. Things had come full circle. It had taken two murders, a false confession, and upstaging the mayor and sheriff, but Aunt Amber finally had her moment of glory.

She wasn't any richer in the pocketbook, though. Rick's claim that Amber was the heir to the Diamond family fortune was bogus, a lie designed to lead the investigation in the wrong direction. He had even forged a new version of Dirk's will to frame Aunt Amber. Tyler had unmasked his lie when he confirmed with Dirk's lawyer. Aunt Amber's non-inheritance was probably all for the best since that amount of money was bound to lead to trouble.

Grandma Vi's ghostly image flitted back and forth, clearly upset. "Why does Amber get all the credit? Maybe Amber brought fame to Westwick Corners, but I'm the one who saved the day."

I looked beside me for Aunt Pearl's reaction, but she had disappeared.

"How, Grandma?" She was even more sensitive as a ghost than she was when alive. Being invisible to everybody except your own family made her insecure, I guess. She felt like nobody noticed her.

"I solved Dirk's murder."

I just stared at her.

"Okay, then. I pointed you to the killer."

"No you didn't," I said. "You just baited me with hints, but you never provided any details. Tyler and I solved both cases on our own."

"How can you say that, Cen? I'm the sole reason that the killer is behind bars."

"By the time you finally told me what you knew, it was too late." I frowned. Grandma had purposely withheld information from a murder investigation. I was still stewing over it. "Besides, you told me there were two people, a man and a woman. That part wasn't true. Rick was the only killer."

"I wasn't about to make it too easy," Grandma Vi snapped. "I wanted to challenge your thinking skills."

"It's not a game, Grandma."

"Let's not fight," Mom said. "All that matters is that Rick Mazure won't hurt anyone ever again. He'll be locked up for a very long time."

"Okay, so maybe you had a small part in solving the case, Cen, but you would never have figured it out without my hints." Grandma's aura turned lavender purple. "In fact, I should be the one receiving accolades, not Amber."

"You're just jealous," Mom said. "Besides, how can anyone possibly give you credit? You're a ghost, remember?"

Grandma Vi looked confused.

"Nobody can see or hear you except for us, Grandma," I pointed out.

Apparently, she hadn't heard us. Grandma Vi crossed her arms. "I just wish everyone would stop ignoring me. I never asked to be invisible. I just wish Amber would give credit where credit is due."

I had never seen Grandma Vi so upset. As a ghost, she couldn't cry, but her apparition wavered and turned a pale bluish color. "I'm really sorry, Grandma. Maybe we can make it up to you somehow?"

Her ghostly form brightened. "Maybe we could go out for a nice family dinner?"

I sighed. Grandma Vi was still coming to terms with her ghostly status. "Sure, why not? You pick the place and I'll make the reservation." Her suggestion was even more ridiculous since ghosts couldn't eat. But I wasn't about to argue with her.

I jumped as something exploded just a few feet away.

I jerked my head in the direction of the boom just as fireworks erupted over my head. The cacophony of sound and light seemed to come from every direction.

I hadn't even noticed her leave, but she was sneaky that way.

Aunt Pearl waved down at us from the City Hall roof. She cackled crazily as she snapped her fingers in tempo with each eruption. A cascade of multi-colored fireworks rained down on us like the Fourth of July.

"No!" Grandma shook her fist at Aunt Pearl. "Stop that, Pearl! Get off the roof before you hurt yourself!"

I rolled my eyes. I should have known that Aunt Pearl would upstage Aunt Amber and that it would somehow involve fire. Their sibling rivalry knew no bounds, and despite Mom being the youngest, she often had to separate them.

"See how it's done, Bill?" Aunt Pearl cried from the roof. "Your props need more pizzazz."

Nobody seemed to hear her above the noise. I was especially glad

Bill couldn't. Otherwise we might end up with another murder on our hands.

I glanced around the crowd. Everyone seemed enraptured with Aunt Amber's speech. Hypnotized, even. I suspect she had cheated with a little witchcraft.

Aunt Amber suddenly stopped mid-speech, confused by the fireworks that clearly were not part of her spell. Aunt Pearl wasn't visible from the City Hall steps, so she must have assumed that the fireworks were part of the celebration.

She just as quickly resumed speaking. "Today is our day to celebrate the lives of two innocent men."

I found my mind drifting as Aunt Amber droned on and on, determined to win as much airtime as possible.

"How did I ever end up with such crazy sisters?" Mom shook her head. "They really need to tone things down a bit and act their age. Amber's making a fool of herself and Pearl's playing with fire."

Crazy or not, at least some good had come from their antics. Aunt Amber had brought movie business to town, which was ultimately good for the Westwick Corners Inn. Despite the tragedy, the Hollywood execs had decided that the show would go on. And they would foot the bill, too. The studio had already lined up new talent for the lead roles, and filming would resume in two weeks.

Without Aunt Amber.

We bought her a ticket to Hawaii.

Aunt Pearl had also discovered an outlet for her pyromania, and I suspected she would apologize to Bill in the hopes he would hire her —again. My aunt never admitted mistakes, so I was quite proud of her. At least she was trying to make a fresh start.

Aunt Amber finished her speech and handed the mic over to Brayden.

It was ever so subtle, but Brayden tapped Tyler on the back. "Thank you, Sheriff Gates, for great police work and keeping us safe. Thanks to your detective work, a ruthless killer is behind bars tonight. We are all thankful."

Grandma Vi was center stage too. She floated across the steps in front of the two men.

I clapped. Mom did the same, and soon others in the crowd followed suit.

"Bravo Ms. West," I shouted.

Grandma Vi beamed. Her transparent form took on a lovely golden sheen as the powerful lights reflected her form. For the moment at least, she remained oblivious to the fact that she was invisible, and that the applause was for Aunt Amber instead.

Aunt Amber noticed it too. She smiled at her mother and walked back towards the microphone. "It's a wrap." She slowly descended the City Hall steps and savored the moment.

Tyler followed a few feet behind, and Grandma Vi floated behind them all as they walked towards us.

Mom sighed. "I never expected real life to be more exciting than a Hollywood movie shoot. Especially not in Westwick Corners."

Aunt Amber whistled "There's No Business Like Show Business" as she approached us.

"You were great up there," I said. "It's a shame the movie never went ahead. I guess it just attracted too much bad luck."

"No, Cen. Witches make their own luck." She winked at me.

"What's that supposed to mean?" I frowned. "Forget it. I don't want to know."

"I hope you've got that acting bug out of your system now, Amber." Mom stifled a yawn. It had been a hectic twenty-four hours.

"Oh, definitely not, Ruby. The best parts are yet to come." Amber smiled, a faraway look in her eyes. "I'm going to be rich and famous. Just you wait and see."

* * *

Love *Witch and Famous*? Get the next book in the series, *Christmas Witch List*

www.colleencross.com

AFTERWORD

If you enjoyed *Witch and Famous,* please recommend it to your friends and leave a short review. It only takes a sentence or two, and word of mouth is an author's best friend!

Witch and Famous is the third book in the *Westwick Witches Cozy Mysteries* series and I have many more books planned. As long as readers like you enjoy my stories, I will continue to write them.

I have also several other mystery and thriller series that you might enjoy. Find out more about my other books at www.colleencross.com.

Want to be the first to know of new releases? Sign up for notifications at www.colleencross.com

Newsletter sign-up form:

http://eepurl.com/bkYx01

You will be sent an email only when I have a new book out.

Thank you for reading my book. I hope you enjoyed reading it as much as I enjoyed writing it! If you liked it, please consider leaving a short review to let others know about my work. Your reviews help me to build readership, which in turn, allows me to keep writing more books.

Thank you so much for reading!

Colleen Cross

ABOUT THE AUTHOR

Mystery and crime thriller author Colleen Cross writes exciting, intelligent thrillers and engrossing mysteries that grip you from the very first page. She took her very own "Exit Strategy" from the corporate world into the book world several years ago to indulge her bookworm wannabe writer self.

Colleen Cross is a retired CPA and CFO who lives with her family on Canada's West Coast. When not writing she loves to run, hike, and explore the coast and mountains with her rescue dog, Jaeger, who reminds her daily that life's too short to not follow your dreams--or a squirrel or two.

Her thriller and mystery books have been translated into multiple languages with more to come. Find them in Dutch, French, German, Italian, Portuguese, Spanish and other languages using search term Colleen Cross

Visit her website at www.colleencross.com and sign up for new release notifications and exclusive subscriber-only offers at http://eepurl.com/bkYx01 or click the QR code below:

Get the latest on Colleen's books here:
www.colleencross.com